Some of the people brought together in this electrifying story of violence and suspense:

HAVILLAND—the brutal detective who conducted investigations with his fists,

JEANNIE—a gorgeous seventeen-year-old blonde with big trouble and nobody to talk to,

BERT KLING—the young patrolman who broke the rules of the police force and tracked down a killer,

CLAIRE—the college girl who had a talent for fast answers and a taste for young boys,

FATS DONNER—gambler, Turkish bath addict, stool pigeon,

EILEEN—the redheaded policewoman who agreed to be bait in a trap set for The Mugger.

THE
MUGGER

By Ed McBain

BALLANTINE BOOKS • NEW YORK

This is for
Angela and Len

Copyright © 1956 by Ed McBain

All rights reserved. Published in the United States by Ballantine Books, a division of Random House, Inc., New York, and simultaneously in Canada by Random House of Canada, Limited, Toronto, Canada.

Library of Congress Catalog Card Number: 56-9704

ISBN 0-345-29290-1

Manufactured in the United States of America

First Edition: November 1975
Second Printing: February 1981

1

The city could be nothing but a woman, and that's good because your business is women.

You know her tossed head in the auburn crowns of molting autumn foliage, Riverhead, and the park. You know the ripe curve of her breast where the River Dix molds it with a flashing bolt of blue silk. Her navel winks at you from the harbor in Bethtown, and you have been intimate with the twin loins of Calm's Point and Majesta. She is a woman, and she is your woman, and in the fall she wears a perfume of mingled wood smoke and carbon dioxide, a musky, musty smell bred of her streets and of her machines and of her people.

You have known her fresh from sleep, clean and un-cluttered. You have seen her naked streets, have heard the sullen murmur of the wind in the concrete canyons of Isola, have watched her come awake, alive, alive.

You have seen her dressed for work, and you have seen her dressed for play, and you have seen her sleek and smooth as a jungle panther at night, her coat glistening with the pinpoint jewels of reflected harbor light. You have known her sultry, and petulant, and loving and hating, and defiant, and meek, and cruel and unjust, and sweet, and poignant. You know all of her moods and all of her ways.

She is big and sprawling and dirty sometimes, and sometimes she shrieks in pain, and sometimes she moans in ecstasy.

But she could be nothing but a woman, and that's good because your business is women.

You are a mugger.

Katherine Ellio sat in a hard, wooden chair in the Detective Squad Room of the 87th Precinct. The early-afternoon sunlight, burnished by autumn, tarnished as a Spanish coin, filtered through the long grilled windows, shadowing her face with a meshed-square pattern.

Her face would not have been a pretty one under any

circumstances. The nose was too long, and the eyes were a washed-out brown, arched with brows that needed plucking. The lips were thin and bloodless, and the chin was sharply pointed. It was not pretty at all now, because someone had discolored her right eye and raised a swollen welt along her jaw line.

"He came up so very suddenly," she said. "I really don't know whether he'd been following me all along or whether he stepped out of an alley. It's hard to say."

Detective 3rd/Grade Roger Havilland looked down at the woman from his six-foot-four height advantage. Havilland owned the body of a wrestler and the face of a Botticelli cherub. He spoke in a loud, heavy voice, not because Miss Ellio was hard of hearing, but simply because Havilland liked to shout.

"Did you hear footsteps?" he shouted.

"I don't remember."

"Miss Ellio, try to remember."

"I am trying."

"All right, was the street dark?"

"Yes."

Hal Willis looked at the woman, and then at Havilland. Willis was a small detective, barely topping the five-foot-eight minimum height requirement. His deceptive height and bone structure, however, gave no clue to the lethal effectiveness with which he pursued his chosen profession. His sparkling, smiling brown eyes added to the misconception of a happy gnome. Even when he was angry, Willis smiled. He was, at the moment, not angry. He was, to be absolutely truthful, simply bored. He had heard this story, or variations of it, many times before. Twelve times, to be exact.

"Miss Ellio," he said, "when did this man hit you?"

"After he took my purse."

"Not before?"

"No."

"How many times did he hit you?"

"Twice."

"Did he say anything to you?"

"Yes, he . . ." Miss Ellio's face contorted with the pain of remembrance. "He said he was only hitting me as a warning. So that I wouldn't scream for help when he left."

2

"What do you think, Rog?" Willis asked. Havilland sighed, and then half shrugged, half nodded.

Willis, in pensive agreement, was silent for a moment. Then he asked, "Did he give you his name, Miss Ellio?"

"Yes," Miss Ellio said. Tears welled up into her inexpressive eyes. "I know this sounds silly. I know you don't believe me. But it's true. I didn't make this up. I —I never had a black eye in my life."

Havilland sighed. Willis was suddenly sympathetic. "Now, now, Miss Ellio," he said, "we believe every word you've told us. You're not the first person who's come to us with this story, you see. We're trying to relate the facts of your experience to the facts we already have." He fished into the breast pocket of his jacket and handed Miss Ellio a handkerchief. "Here now, dry your eyes."

"Thank you," Miss Ellio sobbed. Havilland, bewildered and mystified, blinked at his chivalrous colleague. Willis smiled in his most pleasant A. & P. clerk manner. Miss Ellio, responding immediately, sniffed, dried her eyes, and began to feel as if she were buying a half pound of onions rather than being interrogated on the activities of a mugger.

"Now then," Willis said kindly, "when did he give you his name?"

"After he hit me."

"What did he say?"

"Well, he—he did something first."

"And what was that?"

"He— I know this sounds silly."

Willis smiled reassuringly, radiantly. Miss Ellio lifted her face and smiled back girlishly, and Havilland wondered if perhaps they weren't falling in love.

"Nothing a mugger does sounds silly," Willis said. "Tell us."

"He hit me," Miss Ellio said, "and he warned me, and then he . . . he bowed from the waist." She looked up as if expecting shock and surprise to register on the faces of the detectives. She met level, implacable gazes. "He bowed from the waist," she repeated, as if disappointed with the mild response.

"Yes?" Willis prompted.

"And then he said, 'Clifford thanks you, madam.' "

3

"Well, that figures," Willis said.

"Mmm," Havilland answered noncommittally.

"Clifford thanks you," Miss Ellio repeated. "And then he was gone."

"Did you get any kind of a look at him?" Havilland asked.

"Yes, I did."

"What did he look like?"

"Well . . ." Miss Ellio paused, thinking. "He looked just like anybody else."

Havilland and Willis exchanged patient glances. "Could you be a little more definite?" Willis asked, smiling. "Was he blond? Dark-haired? Redheaded?"

"He was wearing a hat."

"What color were his eyes?"

"He was wearing sunglasses."

"The bright night lights blind him," Havilland said sarcastically. "Either that, or he's come up with a rare eye disease."

"Maybe," Willis said. "Was he clean-shaven? Bearded? Mustached?"

"Yes," Miss Ellio said.

"Which one?" Havilland asked.

"The man who attacked me," she said.

"I meant which one of the thr—"

"Oh. Clean-shaven."

"Long nose or short nose?"

"Well . . . I guess a medium nose."

"Thin lips or fat lips?"

"Medium, I guess."

"Was he short or tall?"

"He was medium height," Miss Ellio said.

"Fat or thin?"

"Medium," she said again.

Willis, somehow, was no longer smiling. Miss Ellio regarded his face, and her own smile disintegrated.

"Well, he was," she said defiantly. "I can't help it if he didn't have a big strawberry mark on his cheek or a mole on his nose or anything. Listen, I didn't ask for him to be an average person. I didn't ask for him to steal my purse, either. There was a lot of money in that bag."

"Well," Havilland shouted, "we'll do what we can to

apprehend him. We have your name and address, Miss Ellio, and if anything comes up we'll notify you. Do you think you'd be able to make a positive identification if you saw the man again?"

"Definitely," Miss Ellio said. "He took a lot of money from me. There was a lot of money in that purse."

Willis bit. "How much, exactly, was in the purse?" he asked.

"Nine dollars and seventy-two cents," Miss Ellio answered.

"Plus a fortune in rare gems," Havilland added in one of his choicer attempts at wit.

"What?" Miss Ellio said.

"We'll call you," Havilland answered, and he took her elbow and escorted her to the slatted railing that divided the Squad Room from the corridor. When he got back to the desk, Willis was doodling on a sheet of paper.

"Nude broads again?" Havilland asked.

"What?"

"You're a sex fiend."

"I know. But I'm big enough to admit it. What do you make of Miss Ellio?"

"I think she invented the story."

"Come on, Rog."

"I think she's been reading in the newspapers about the mugger named Clifford. I think she's an old maid who lives in a two-room apartment. I think she looks under the bed every night and finds nothing but the chamber pot. I think she tripped over the chamber pot last night, bruised herself, and decided to make a bid for a little excitement." Havilland caught his breath. "I also think you and her would make a good couple. Why don't you ask her to marry you?"

"You're very comical on Tuesdays," Willis said. "You don't believe she was mugged?"

"The sunglasses part was a stroke of real genius! Jesus, the lengths people will go to when they're lying."

"He *may* have been wearing sunglasses," Willis said.

"Sure. And Bermuda shorts, too. Like I said, he's suddenly contracted pink eye." Havilland snorted. " 'Clifford thanks you, madam.' Straight out of the papers. There ain't a citizen of this city who hasn't heard

5

about Cliff the Mugger and his punch in the mouth and his bow from the waist."

"I think she was telling the truth," Willis said.

"Then you type up the report," Havilland answered. "Just between you and me, Cliff's beginning to give me a big pain in the ass."

Willis stared at Havilland.

"What's the matter?" Havilland shouted.

"When's the last time you typed up a report?"

"Who wants to know?"

"I do," Willis said.

"When did you become police commissioner?"

"I don't like the way you goof off," Willis answered. He wheeled over the typing cart, opened the desk drawer, and took out three sheets of the DD report form.

"Everybody else is goofing off, ain't they?" Havilland asked. "What's Carella doing, if not goofing off?"

"He's on his honeymoon, for Christ's sake," Willis said.

"So? What kind of an excuse is that? I say this Ellio broad is a nut. I say this doesn't call for a report. I say if you feel like typing one up, go ahead."

"Do you feel strong enough to take another look at the Lousy File?"

"Under what?" Havilland mocked. "Muggers named Clifford who wear sunglasses and Bermuda shorts?"

"We may have missed something," Willis said. "Of course, the cabinet's at least four feet away. I don't want you to strain yourself."

"I been through the file and back again," Havilland said. "Every time this Clifford character hits another broad. There's nothing, nothing. And what this Ellio broad gave us ain't gonna add one bit to the picture."

"It might," Willis said.

"No," Havilland said, shaking his head. "And you know why? Because that mugging didn't take place in the street, like she said it did."

"No? Then where did it take place?"

"In her head, pal," Havilland said. "All in Miss Ellio's head."

6

2

The shoulder didn't hurt at all now.

It was funny. You figure you get shot in the shoulder, it's going to hurt for a long long time. But it didn't. Not at all.

As a matter of fact, if Bert Kling had had his way, he'd be back on the job, and that job was working as a patrolman out of the 87th Precinct. But Captain Frick was the boss of the uniformed cops at the house, and Captain Frick had said, "Now you take another week, Bert. I don't care whether the hospital let you go or not. You take another week."

And so Bert Kling was taking another week, and not enjoying it very much. "Another week" had started with Monday, and this was Tuesday, and it seemed like a nice brisk autumn day outside and Kling had always liked autumn, but he was bored silly with it now.

The hospital duty hadn't been bad in the beginning. The other cops had come up to see him, and even some of the detectives had dropped around, and he'd been something of a precinct celebrity, getting shot up like that. But after a while, he had ceased to be a novelty, and the visits had been less frequent, and he had leaned back against the fat hospital mattress and begun his adjustment to the boredom of convalescence.

His favorite indoor sport had become the crossing off of days on the calendar. He had also ogled the nurses, but the joy of such diversion had evaporated when he had realized his activities—so long as he was a patient, at any rate—could never rise higher that the spectator level. So he had crossed off the days, one by one, and he had looked forward to returning to the job, yearned for it with almost ferocious intensity.

And then Frick had said, "Take another week, Bert."

He'd wanted to say, "Now look, Captain, I don't need any more rest. I'm as strong as an ox. Believe me, I can handle *two* beats."

But knowing Frick, and knowing he was a thickheaded old jerk, Kling had kept his peace. He was still keeping his peace. He was very tired of keeping his peace. It was almost better getting shot.

Now that was curious attitude, he realized, wanting to get back to the job which had been responsible for the bullet in his right shoulder. Not that he'd been shot doing his job, actually. He'd been shot off duty, coming out of a bar, and he wouldn't have been shot if he hadn't been mistaken for someone else.

The shot had been intended for a reporter named Savage, a reporter who'd done some snooping around, a reporter who'd asked too many leading questions of a teen-age gang member who'd later summoned all his pals and colleagues to the task of taking care of Savage.

It happened to be Kling's misfortune that he'd been coming out of the same bar in which Savage had earlier interrogated the kid. It was also his misfortune that he was blond, because Savage, inconsiderately, was blond, too. The kids had jumped Kling, anxious to mete out justice, and Kling had pulled his service revolver from his back pocket.

And that's how heroes are made.

Kling shrugged.

Even when he shrugged, the shoulder didn't hurt. So why should he be sitting here in a stupid furnished room when he could be out walking a beat?

He rose and walked to the window, looking down toward the street. The girls were having trouble keeping their skirts tucked against the strong wind. Kling watched.

He liked girls. He liked all girls. Walking his beat, he would watch the girls. He always felt pleased when he did. He was twenty-four-years old, and a veteran of the Korean fracas, and he could remember the women he'd seen there, but he never once connected those women with the pleasure he felt in watching the girls in America.

He had seen women crouched in the mud, their cheeks gaunt, their eyes glowing with the reflected light of napalm infernos, wide with terror at the swishing roar of the jet bombers. He had seen underfed bodies hung with baggy quilted garments. He had seen women nurs-

8

ing babies, breasts exposed. The breasts should have been ripe and full with nourishment. They had been, instead, puckered and dried—withered fruits clinging to starved vines.

He had seen young women and old women clawing in the rubble for food, and he could still remember the muted, begging faces and the hollow eyes.

And now, he watched the girls. He watched the strong legs, and the firm breasts, and the well-rounded buttocks, and he felt good. Maybe he was crazy, but there was something exhilarating about strong white teeth and sun-tanned faces and sun-bleached hair. Somehow, they made *him* feel strong, too, and maybe he was crazy, and never once did he make any connection with what he had seen in Korea.

The knock on the door startled him. He whirled from the window and called, "Who is it?"

"Me," the voice answered. "Peter."

"Who?" he asked.

"Peter. Peter Bell."

Who's Peter Bell? he wondered. He shrugged and went to the dresser. He opened the top drawer and took his .38 from where it lay alongside a box holding his tie clasps. With the gun dangling at his side, he walked to the door and opened it a crack. A man can get shot only once before he realizes you don't open doors too wide, even when the man outside has already given his name.

"Bert?" a voice said. "This is Peter Bell. Open the door."

"I don't think I know you," Kling said cautiously, peering into the darkened hallway, half expecting a volley of shots to splinter the door's wood.

"You don't *know* me? Hey, kid, this is Peter. Hey, don't you remember me? When we were kids? Up in Riverhead? This is me. Peter Bell."

Kling opened the door a little wider. The man standing in the hallway was no older than twenty-seven. He was tall and muscularly built. He wore a brown leather jacket and yachting cap. In the dimness, Kling could not make out his features clearly, but there was something familiar in the face and he began to feel a little foolish holding a gun. He swung the door open.

"Come in," he said.

Peter Bell walked into the room. He saw the gun almost instantly, and his eyes went wide. "Hey!" he said. "Hey, Jesus, Bert, what's the matter?"

Holding the gun loosely, finally recognizing the man who stood before him in the center of the room, Kling felt immensely ridiculous. He smiled sheepishly. "I was cleaning it," he said.

"You do recognize me now?" Bell asked, and Kling had the distinct impression that his lie had not been accepted.

"Yes," he said. "How are you, Peter?"

"Oh, soso, can't kick." He extended his hand, and Kling took it, studying his face more carefully in the light of the room. Bell would have been a good-looking man were it not for the prominence and structure of his nose. In fact, if there was any one part of the face Kling did not recognize, it was the massive, craggy structure that protruded incongruously between sensitive brown eyes. Peter Bell, he remembered now, had been an extremely handsome youth, and he imagined the nose had been one of those things which, during adolesence, simply grow on you. The last time he'd seen Bell had been fifteen years ago, when Bell had moved to another section of Riverhead. The nose, then, had been acquired sometime during that span of years. He realized abruptly that he was staring at the protuberance, and his discomfort increased when Bell said, "Some schnoz, huh? Eeek, what a beak! Is it a nose or a hose?"

Kling chose that point in the conversation to return his revolver to the open dresser drawer.

"I guess you're wondering what I want," Bell said.

Kling was, in truth, wondering just that. He turned from the dresser and said, "Well, no. Old friends often . . . He stopped, unable to complete the lie. He did not consider Peter Bell a friend. He had not laid eyes on him for fifteen years, and even when they'd been boys together, they'd never been particularly close.

"I read in the papers where you got shot," Bell said. "I'm a big reader. I buy six newspapers every day. How do you like that? Bet you didn't even know there was six papers in this city. I read them all, cover to cover. Never miss anything."

Kling smiled, not knowing what to say.

"Yes, sir," Bell went on, "and it certainly came as a shock to me and Molly when we read you got shot. I ran into your mother on Forrest Avenue a little while after that. She said her and your dad were very upset about it, but that's to be expected."

"Well, it was only a shoulder wound," Kling said.

"Only a scratch, huh?" Bell said, grinning. "Well, I got to hand it to you, kid."

"You said Forrest Avenue. Have you moved back to the old neighborhood?"

"Huh? Oh, no, no. I'm a hackie now. Got my own cab, medallion and everything. I usually operate in Isola, but I had a Riverhead call, and that's how I happened to be on Forrest Avenue, and that's how I happened to spot your mom. Yeah, sure."

Kling looked at Bell again, realizing the "yachting cap" was simply his working headgear.

"I read in the papers where the hero cop got discharged from the hospital," Bell said. "Gave your address and everything. You don't live with the folks no more, huh?"

"No," Kling said. "When I got back from Korea. . . ."

"I missed that one," Bell said. Punctured eardrum, how's that for a laugh? I think the real reason they rejected me was because of the schnoz." He touched his nose. "So the papers said where your commanding officer ordered you to take another week's rest." Bell smiled. His teeth were very white and very even. There was an enviable cleft in his chin. *It's too bad about the nose,* Kling thought. "How does it feel being a celebrity? Next thing you know, you'll be on that television show, answering questions about Shakespeare."

"Well . . ." Kling said weakly. He was beginning to wish that Peter Bell would go away. He had not asked for the intrusion, and he was finding it tiresome.

"Yep," Bell said, "I certainly got to hand it to you, kid." and then a heavy silence fell over the room.

Kling bore the silence as long as he was able. "Would you like a drink . . . or anything?" he asked.

"Never touch it," Bell said.

The silence returned.

Bell touched his nose again. "The reason I'm here," he said at last.

11

"Yes?" Kling prompted.

"Tell you the truth, I'm a little embarrassed, but Molly figured—" Bell stopped. "I'm married now, you know."

"I didn't know."

"Yeah. Molly. Wonderful woman. Got two kids, another on the way."

"That's nice," Kling said, his feeling of awkwardness increasing.

"Well I might as well get right down to it. huh? Molly's got a sister, nice kid. Her name is Jeannie. She's seventeen. She's been living with us ever since Molly's mom died—two years now, it must be. Yeah." Bell stopped.

"I see," Kling said, wondering what Bell's marital life had to do with him.

"The kid's pretty. Look, I might as well level with you, she's a knockout. Matter of fact, she looks just the way Molly looked when she was that age, and Molly's no slouch—even now, pregnant and all."

"I don't understand, Peter."

"Well, the kid's been running around."

"Running around?"

"Well that's what Molly thinks, anyway." Bell seemed suddenly uncomfortable. "You know, she doesn't see her dating any of the local kids or anything, and she knows the kid goes out, so she's afraid she's in with the wrong crowd, do you know what I mean? It wouldn't be so bad if Jeannie wasn't such a pretty kid, but she is. I mean look, Bert, I'll level with you. She's my sister-in-law and all that, but she's got it all over a lot of older dames you see around. Believe me, she's a knockout."

"Okay," Kling said.

"So Jeannie won't tell us anything. We talk to her until we're blue in the face, and we don't get a peep out of her. Molly got the idea of getting a private detective to follow her, see where she goes, that kind of thing. Bert, on the money I make, I can't afford a private dick. Besides, I don't really think the kid is doing anything wrong."

"You want *me* to follow her?" Kling asked, suddenly getting the picture.

12

"No, no, nothing like that. Jesus, would I come ask a favor like that after fifteen years? No, Bert, no."

"What then?"

"I want you to talk to her. That way, Molly'll be happy. Look, Bert, when a woman is carrying, she gets goofy ideas. Pickles and ice cream, you know? Okay, so this is the same thing. She's got this nutty idea that Jeannie is a juvenile delinquent or something."

"*Me* talk to her? Kling was flabbergasted, "I don't even know her. What good would it do for me to—"

"You're a cop. Molly respects law and order. If I bring a cop around, she'll be happy."

"Hell, I'm practically still a rookie."

"Sure, but that don't matter. Molly'll see the uniform and be happy. Besides, you really might help Jeannie, Who knows? I mean if she *is* involved with some young toughs."

"No, I couldn't, Peter. I'm sorry, but—"

"You got a whole week ahead of you," Bell said, "nothing to do. Look, Bert, I read the papers. Would I ask you to give up any spare time if I knew you were pounding a beat during the day? Bert, give me credit."

"That's not it, Peter. I wouldn't know what to say to the girl. I just—I don't think so."

"Please, Bert. As a personal favor to me. For old time's sake what do you say?"

"No," Kling answered.

"There's a chance, too, she *is* in with some crumbs. What then? Ain't a cop supposed to prevent crime, nip it in the bud? You're a big disappointment to me, Bert."

"I'm sorry."

"Okay, okay, no hard feelings," Bell said. He rose, seemingly ready to go. "If you should change your mind, though, I'll leave my address with you." He took his wallet out of his pocket and fished for a scrap of paper.

"There's no sense . . ."

"Just in case you should change your mind," Bell said. "Here, now." He took a pencil stub from the pocket of the leather jacket and began scribbling on the paper scrap. "It's on De Witt Street, the big house in the middle of the block. You can't miss it. If you should

13

change your mind, come around tomorrow night. I'll keep Jeannie home until nine o'clock. Okay?"

"I don't think I'll change my mind," Kling said.

"If you should," Bell answered. "I'd appreciate it, Bert. That's tomorrow night. Wednesday. Okay? Here's the address." He handed Bert the paper. "I put the telephone number down, too, in case you should get lost. You better put it in your wallet."

Kling took the paper, and then, because Bell was watching him so closely, he put it into his wallet.

"I hope you come," Bell said. He walked to the door. "Thanks for listening to me, anyway. It was good seeing you again, Bert."

"Yes," Kling said.

"So long now. Bell closed the door behind him. The room was suddenly quiet.

Kling went to the window. He saw Bell when he emerged from the building. He watched as Bell climbed into a green-and-yellow taxicab and then gunned away from the curb. The cab had been parked alongside a fire hydrant.

3

They write songs about Saturday night.

The songs all promote the idea that Saturday is a particularly lonely night. The myth has become a part of American culture, and everybody is familiar with it. Stop anybody, six to sixty, and ask, "What's the loneliest night of the week?" and the answer you'll get is "Saturday."

Well, Tuesday's not such a prize, either.

Tuesday hasn't had the benefit of press agentry and promotion, and nobody's written a song about Tuesday. But to a lot of people, the Saturday nights and the Tuesday nights are one and the same. You can't estimate degrees of loneliness. Who is more lonely, a man on a desert island on a Saturday night, or a woman carrying a torch in the biggest, noisiest night club on a Tuesday night? Loneliness doesn't respect the calender. Saturday,

14

Tuesday, Friday, Thursday—they're all the same, and they're all gray.

On Tuesday night, September 12, a black Mercury sedan was parked on one of the city's loneliest streets, and the two men sitting on the front seat were doing one of the world's loneliest jobs.

In Los Angeles, they call this job "stakeout." In the city for which these two men worked, the job was known as "a plant."

A plant requires a certain immunity to sleepfulness, a definite immunity to loneliness, and a good deal of patience.

Of the two men sitting in the Mercury sedan, Detective 2nd/Grade Meyer was the more patient. He was, in fact, the most patient cop in the 87th Precinct, if not the entire city. Meyer had a father who considered himself a very humorous man. His father's name was Max. When Meyer was born, Max named him Meyer. This was considered convulsively comic, a kid named Meyer Meyer. You had to be very patient if you're born a Jew to begin with. You have to be supernaturally patient if your hilarious old man tags you with a handle like Meyer Meyer. He was patient. But a lifelong devotion to patience often provides a strain and, as the saying goes, something's got to give. Meyer Meyer was as bald as a cue ball, even though he was only thirty-seven years old.

Detective 3rd/Grade Temple was falling asleep. Meyer could always tell when Temple was ready to conk off. Temple was a giant of a man, and big men needed more sleep, Meyer supposed.

"Hey!" he said.

Temple's shaggy brows shot up onto his forehead. "What's the matter?"

"Nothing. What do you think of a mugger who calls himself Clifford?"

"I think he should be shot," Temple said. He turned and faced the penetrating stare of Meyer's mild blue eyes.

"I think so, too," Meyer said, smiling. "You awake?"

"I'm awake." Temple scratched his crotch. "I've had this damn itch for the past three days. Drives me nuts. You can't scratch it in public, either."

15

"Jungle Rot," Meyer said.

"Something like that. Jesus, it's ruining me." He paused. "My wife won't come near me. She's afraid she'll catch it."

"Maybe she *gave* it to you," Meyer suggested.

Temple yawned. "I never thought of that. Maybe she did." He scratched himself again.

"If I were a mugger," Meyer said, figuring the only way to keep Temple awake was to talk to him, "I wouldn't pick a name like Clifford."

"Clifford sounds like a pansy," Temple agreed.

"Steve is a good name for a mugger," Meyer said.

"Don't let Carella hear you say that."

"But Clifford. I don't know. You think it's his real name?"

"It could be. Why bother giving it, if it's not his real name?"

"That's a point," Meyer said.

"I got him tabbed as a psycho, anyway," Temple said. "Who else would take a deep bow and then thank his victim? He's a screwball."

"Do you know the one about the headline?" Meyer, a man who was fond of a good joke, asked.

"No. What's that?"

"The headline they put on the newspaper when this maniac escaped from an insane asylum, ran for three miles, and then raped a neighborhood girl?"

"No," Temple said. "What was the headline?"

Meyer spelled it out grandly with his hands.

"NUTS! BOLTS AND SCREWS!"

"You and your jokes," Temple said. "Sometimes I think you enjoy these damn plants."

"Sure, I love them."

"Well, phycho or not, he's knocked over thirteen so far. Did Willis tell you about the dame who came in this afternoon?"

Meyer glanced at his watch. "*Yesterday* afternoon," he corrected. "Yes, he told me. Maybe thirteen'll be Cliff's unlucky number, huh?"

"Yeah, maybe. I don't like muggers, you know? They

give me a pain." He scratched himself. "I like gentlemen thieves."

"Like what?"

"Like murderers even. Murderers, it seems to me, have more class than muggers."

"Give Cliff time," Meyer said. "He's still warming up."

Both men fell silent. Meyer seemed to be getting something straight in his mind. At last, he said, "I've been following this case in the papers. One of the other precincts. Thirty-third, I think."

"Yeah, what about it?"

"Some guy's going around stealing cats."

"Yeah?" Temple asked. "You mean cats?"

"Yeah," Meyer said, watching Temple closely. "You know, house pets. So far, they've had eighteen squeals on it in the past week. Something, huh?"

"I'll say," Temple said.

"I've been following it," Meyer said. "I'll let you know how it turns out." He kept watching Temple, a twinkle in his blue eyes. Meyer was a very patient man. If he'd told Temple about the kidnaped cats, he'd done so for a very good reason. He was still watching Temple when he saw him sit suddenly erect.

"What?" he said.

"Shhh!" Temple said.

They listened together. From far off down the darkened street, they could hear the steady clatter of a woman's high-heeled shoes on the pavement. The city was silent around them, like an immense cathedral closed for the night. Only the hollow, piercing chatter of the wooden heels broke the stillness. They sat in silence, waiting, watching.

The girl went past the car, not turning her head to look at it. She walked quickly, her head high. She was in her early thirties, a tall girl with long blond hair. She swept past the car, and the sound of her heels faded, and still the men were silent, listening.

The even cadence of a second pair of heels came to them. Not the light, empty chatter a woman's feet make. This was heavy conversation. These were the footsteps of a man.

"Clifford?" Temple asked.

17

"Maybe."

They waited. The footsteps came closer. They watched the man approaching in the rearview mirror. Then, simultaneously, both Temple and Meyer stepped out of the car from opposite sides.

The man stopped, fright darting into his eyes.

"What—" he said. "What is this? A holdup?"

Meyer cut around behind the car and came up alongside of the man. Temple was already blocking his path.

"Your name Clifford?" Temple asked.

"Wah?"

"Clifford."

"No," the man said, shaking his head violently. "You got the wrong party. Look, I—"

"Police," Temple said tersely, and he flashed the tin.

"P—p—police? What'd I do?"

"Where're you going?" Meyer asked.

"Home. I just come from a movie."

"Little late to be getting out of a movie, isn't it?"

"Wah? Oh, yeah, we stopped in a bar."

"Where do you live?"

"Right down the street." The man pointed, perplexed, frightened.

"What's your name?"

"Frankie's my name." He paused. "Ask anybody."

"Frankie what?"

"Oroglio. With a *g*."

"What were you doing following that girl?" Meyer shot.

"Wah? Girl? Hey, whatta you nuts or something?"

"You were following a girl!" Temple said. "Why?"

"Me?" Oroglio pointed both hands at his chest. "Me? Hey, listen, you made a mistake, fellers. I mean it. You got the wrong guy."

"A blonde just walked down this street," Temple said, "and you came along behind her. If you weren't following—"

"A blonde? Oh, Jesus," Oroglio said.

"Yes, a blonde," Temple said, his voice rising. "Now how about it, mister?"

"In a blue coat?" Oroglio asked. "Like in a little blue coat? Is that who you mean?"

"That's who we mean," Temple said.

"Oh, Jesus," Oroglio said.

"HOW ABOUT IT?" Temple shouted.

"That's my wife!"

"What?"

"My wife, my wife. Conchetta." Oroglio was wagging his head wildly now. "My wife, Conchetta. She ain't no blonde. She bleaches it."

"Look, mister."

"I swear. We went to the snow together, and then we stopped for a few beers. We had a fight in the bar. So she walked out alone. She always does that. She's nuts."

"Yeah?" Meyer said.

"I swear on my Aunt Christina's hair. She blows up, and she takes off, and I give her four, five minutes. Then I follow her. That's all there is to it. Jesus, I wouldn't follow no blonde."

Temple looked at Meyer.

"I'll take you up to the house," Oroglio said, plunging on. "I'll introduce you. She's my wife! Listen, what do you want? She's my wife!"

"I'll bet she is," Meyer said resignedly. Patiently, he turned to Temple. "Go back to the car, George," he said. "I'll check this out."

Oroglio sighed. "Gee, this is kind of funny, you know that?" he said relieved. "I mean being accused of following my own wife. It's kind of funny."

"It could've been funnier," Meyer said.

"Yeah? How?"

"She could've been somebody else's wife."

He stood in the shadows of the alley, wearing the night like a cloak. He could hear his own shallow breathing and beyond that the vast murmur of the city, the murmur of a big-bellied woman in sleep. There were lights in some of the apartments, solitary sentinels piercing the blackness with unblinking yellow. It was dark where he stood, though, and the darkness was a friend to him, and they stood shoulder to shoulder. Only his eyes glowed in the darkness, watching, waiting,

He saw the woman long before she crossed the street. She was wearing flats, rubber-soled and rubber-heeled, and she made no sound, but he saw her instantly and he tensed himself against the sooty brick wall of the

19

building, waiting, studying her, watching the careless way in which she carried her purse.

She looked athletic, this one.

A beer barrel with squat legs. He liked them better when they looked feminine. This one didn't wear high heels, and there was a springy bounce to her walk; she was probably one of these walkers, one of these girls who do six miles before breakfast. She was closer now, still with that bounce in her step as if she were on a pogo stick. She was grinning, too, grinning like a big baboon picking lice; maybe she was coming home from bingo, or maybe a poker session; maybe she'd just made a big killing, and maybe this big bouncing baby's bag was just crammed full of juicy bills.

He reached out.

His arm circled her neck, and he pulled her to him before she could scream, yanking her into the blackened mouth of the alley. He swung her around then, releasing her neck, catching sweater up in one big hand, holding it bunched in his fist, slamming her against the brick wall of the building.

"Quiet," he said. His voice was very low. He looked at her face. She had hard green eyes, and the eyes were narrow now, watching him. She had a thick nose and leathery skin.

"What do you want from me?" she asked. Her voice was gruff.

"Your purse," he answered. "Quick."

"Why are you wearing sunglasses?"

"Give me your purse!"

He reached for it, and she swung it away from him. His tightened on the sweater. He pulled her off the wall for an instant, and then slammed her back against the bricks again. "The purse!"

"No!"

He bunched his left fist and hurled it at her mouth. The woman's head rocked back. She shook it, dazed.

"Listen," he said, "listen to me. I don't want to hurt you, you hear? That was just a warning. Now give me the purse, and don't make a peep after I'm gone, you hear? Not a peep!"

The woman slowly wiped the back of her hand across her mouth. She looked at the blood in the darkness, and then she hissed, "Don't touch me again, you punk!"

He brought back his fist. She kicked him suddenly, and he bent over in pain. She struck out at his face, her fleshy fists bunched, hitting him over and over again.

"You stupid—" he started, and then he caught her hands and shoved her back against the wall. He hit her twice, feeling his bunched knuckles smashing into her stupid, ugly face. She fell back against the wall, moaned, and then collapsed to the concrete at his feet.

He stood over her, breathing heavily. He looked over his shoulder, staring off down the street, lifting the sunglasses for a better view. There was no one in sight. Hastily, he bent down and retrieved the purse from where it had fallen.

The woman did not move.

He looked at her again, wondering. Dammit, why had she been so stupid? He hadn't wanted this to happen. He bent down again, and he put his head on her bosom. Her breast was hard, like a man's pectorals, but she was breathing. He rose, sastisfied, and a small smile flitted across his face.

He stood over her, and he bowed, the hand with the purse crossing his waist gallantly, and he said, "Clifford thanks you, madam."

And then he ran into the night.

4

The bulls of the 87th Squad, no matter what else they agreed upon, generally disagreed upon the comparitive worth of the various stool pigeons they employed from time to time. For as the old maid remarked upon kissing the cow, "It's all a matter of taste," and one cop's pigeon might very well be another cop's poison.

It was generally conceded that Danny Gimp was the most trustworthy of the lot, but even Danny's stanchest supporters realized that some of their colleagues got better results from some of the other birds. That all of them relied heavily upon information garnered from underworld contacts was an undisputed fact; it was simply a question of whom you preferred to use.

Hal Willis favored a man named Fats Donner.

In fact, with Donner's solicited and recompensed aid, he had cracked many a tough nut straight down the middle. And there was no question but what Clifford, the mugger with the courtly bow, was beginning to be a tough nut.

There was only one drawback to using Donner, and that was his penchant for Turkish baths. Willis was a thin man. He did not enjoy losing three or four pounds whenever he asked Donner a question.

Donner, on the other hand, was not only fat; he was Fats. And Fats, for the benefit of the uninitiated, is "fat" in the plural. He was obese. He was immense. He was mountainous.

He sat with a towel draped across his crotch, the thick layers of flesh quivering everywhere on his body as he sucked in the steam that surrounded him and Willis. His body was a pale, sickly white, and Willis suspected he was a junkie, but he'd be damned if he'd pull in a good pigeon on a holding rap.

Donner sat, a great white Buddha, sucking in steam. Willis watched him, sweating.

"Clifford, huh?" Donner asked. His voice was a deep, sepulchral rattle, as if Death were his silent partner.

"Clifford," Willis said. He could feel the perspiration seeping up into his close-cropped hair, could feel it trickling down the back of his neck, over his narrow shoulders, across his naked backbone. He was hot. His mouth was dry. He watched Donner languishing like a huge, contented vegetable and he cursed all fat men, and he said, "Clifford. You must have read about him. It's in all the papers."

"I don't dig papers, man," Donner said. "Only the funnies."

"Okay, he's a mugger. He slams his victims before he takes off, then he bows from the waist and says, 'Clifford thanks you, madam.'"

"Only chicks this guy taps?"

"So far," Willis said.

"I don't make him, dad," Donner said, shaking his

22

head, sprinkling sweat onto the tiled walls around him. "Clifford. The name's from nowhere. Hit me again."

"He wears sunglasses. Last two times out, anyway."

"Cheaters? He flies by night, this cat?"

"Yes?"

"Clifford, chicks, cheaters. All *C*'s. A cokie?"

"We don't know."

"*C*, you dig me?" Donner said. "Clifford, chicks . . ."

"I caught it the first time around," Willis answered.

Donner shrugged. It seemed to be getting hotter in the steam room. The steam billowed up from hidden instruments of the devil, smothering the room with a thick blanket of soggy, heat-laden mist. Willis sighed heavily.

"Clifford," Donner said again. "This his square handle?"

"I don't know."

"I mean, dad, I grip with a few muggers, but none with a Clifford tag. If this is just a party stunt to gas the chicks, that's another thing again. Still, Clifford. This he picked from hunger."

"He's knocked over fourteen women," Willis said. "He's not so hungry any more."

"Rape?"

"No."

"No eyes for the chicks, this Clifford cat, huh? He's a faggot?"

"We don't know."

"Big hauls?"

"Fifty-four bucks was tops. Mostly peanuts."

"Small time," Donner said.

"Do you know any *big-time* muggers?

"The ones who work the Hill don't go for chewing-gum loot. I've known plenty big time muggers in my day." Donner lay back on the marble seat, readjusting the towel across his middle. Willis wiped sweat from his face with a sweaty hand.

"Listen, don't you ever conduct business outside?" Willis asked.

"What do you mean, outside?"

"Where there's air."

"Oh. Sure, I do. This summer I was out a lot. Man, it was a great summer, wasn't it?"

Willis thought of the record-breaking temperatures

23

that had crippled the back of the city. "Yeah, great," he said. "So what about this, Fats? Have you got anything for me?"

"No rumble, if that's what you mean. He's either new, or he keeps still."

"Many new faces in town?"

"Always new faces, dad," Donner said. "None I peg for muggers, though. Tell the truth, I don't know many hit-and-run boys. This is for the wet-pants nowadays. You figure Clifford for a kid?"

"Not from what the victims have told us about him."

"Old man?"

"Twenties."

"Tough age," Donner said. "Not quite a boy, yet not quite a man."

"He hits like a man," Willis said. "He sent the one last night to the hospital."

"I tell you, Donner said, "let me go on the earie. I listen a little here and there, and I buzz you. Dig?"

"When?" Willis asked.

"Soon."

"How soon is soon?"

"How high is up?" Donner asked. He rubbed his nose with his forefinger. "You looking for a lead or a pinch?"

"A lead would suit me fine," Willis said.

"Gone. So let me sniff a little. What's today?"

"Wednesday,"Willis said.

"Wednesday," Donner repeated, and then for some reason, he added, "Wednesday's a good day. I'll try to get back to you sometime tonight."

"If you'll call, I'll wait for it. Otherwise, I go home at four."

"I'll call," Donner promised.

"Hey, ain't you forgetting something?" Donner called.

Willis turned. "All I came in with was the towel," he said.

"Yeah, but I come in here every day, man," Donner said. "This can cost a man, you know."

"We'll talk cost when you deliver," Willis said. "All I got so far is a lot of hot air."

Bert Kling wondered what he was doing here.

He came down the steps from the elevated structure,

and he recognized landmarks instantly. This had not been his old neighborhood, but he had listed this area among his teen-age stamping grounds and he was surprised now to find a faint nostalgia creeping into his chest.

If he looked off down the Avenue, he could see the wide sweep of the train tracks where the El screeched sparkingly around Cannon Road, heading north. He could see, too, the flickering lights of a Ferris wheel against the deepening sky—the carnival, every September and every April, rain or shine, setting up business in the empty lot across from the housing project. He had gone to the carnival often when he was a kid, and he knew this section of Riverhead as well as he knew his own old neighborhood. Both were curious mixtures of Italians, Jews, Irish, and Negroes. Somebody had set a pot to melting in Riverhead, and somebody else had forgotten to turn off the gas.

There had never been a racial or religious riot in this section of the city, and Kling doubted if there ever would be one. He could remember back to 1935 and the race riots in Diamondback, and the way the people in Riverhead had wondered if the riots would spread there, too. It was certainly a curiously paradoxical thing; for while white men and black men were slitting each other's throats in Diamondback, white men and black men in Riverhead prayed together that the disease would not spread to their community.

He was only a little boy at the time, but he could still remember his father's words: "If you help spread any of this filth, you won't be able to sit for a week, Bert. I'll fix you so you'll be lucky if you can even *walk!*"

The disease had not spread.

He walked up the Avenue now, drinking in the familiar landmarks. The *latticini*, and the kosher butcher shop, and the paint store, and the big A. & P., and the bakeshop, and Sam's candy store there on the corner. God, how many ice-cream sundaes had he eaten in Sam's? He was tempted to stop in and say Hello, but he saw a stranger behind the counter, a short, bald-headed man, not Sam at all, and he realized with painful clarity that a lot of things had changed since he was a carefree adolescent.

25

The thought was sobering as well as painful, and he wondered for the fiftieth time why he had come back to Riverhead, why he was walking toward De Witt Street and the home of Peter Bell. To talk to a young girl? What could he say to a seventeen-year-old kid? Keep your legs crossed, honey?

He shrugged his wide shoulders. He was a tall man, and he was wearing his dark-blue suit tonight, and his blond hair seemed blonder against the dark fabric. When he reached De Witt, he turned south and then reached into his wallet for the address Peter had given him. Up the street, he could see the yellow brick and the cyclone fence of the junior high school. The street was lined with private houses, mostly wooden structures, here and there a brick dwelling tossed in to break the monotomy. Old trees grew close to the curbs on either side of the street, arching over the street to embrace in a blazing, autumn-leaved cathedral. There was something very quiet and very peaceful about De Witt Street. He saw the bushels of leaves piled near the gutter, saw a man standing with a rake in one hand, the other hand on his hip, solemnly watching the small, smoky fire of leaves burning at his feet. The smell was a good one. He sucked it in deep into his lungs. This was a lot different from the crowded, bulging streets the 87th Precinct presided over. This was a lot different from crowded tenements and soot-stained buildings reaching grimy concrete fingers to the sky. The trees here were of the same species found in Grover's Park, which hemmed in the 87th on the south. But you could be sure no assassins lurked behind their stout trunks. That was the difference.

In the deepening dusk, with the street lamps going on suddenly, Bert Kling walked and listened to the sound of his footsteps and—quite curiously—he was glad he had come.

He found Bell's house: the big one in the middle of the block, just as he'd promised. It was a tall, two-family, clapboard-and-brick structure, the clapboard white. A rutted concrete driveway sloped upward toward a white garage at the back of the house. A flight of steps led to the front door. Kling checked the address again, and then climbed the steps and pressed the bell button set in the doorjamb. He waited a second, and the door buzzed, and he heard the small click as he twisted the knob and shoved it inward. He was in a small foyer, and he saw another door open instantly, and then Peter Bell stepped into the foyer, grinning.

"Bert, you came! Jesus, I don't know how to thank you."

Kling nodded and smiled. Bell took his hand.

"Come in, come in." His voice dropped to a whisper. "Jeannie's still here. I'll introduce you as a cop friend of mine, and then Molly and me'll take off, okay?"

"Okay," Kling said. Bell led him to the open doorway. There were still cooking smells in the house, savory smells that heightened Kling's feeling of nostalgia. The house was warm and secure, welcome after the slight nip there had been in the air outside.

Bell closed the door and called, "Molly!"

The house, Kling saw immediately, was constructed like a railroad flat, one room following the other, so that you had to walk through every room in the house if you wanted to get to the end room. The front door opened into the living room, a small room furnished with a three-piece sofa-and-easy-chair set that had undoubtedly been advertised as a "Living Room Suite" by one of the cheaper furniture stores. There was a mirror on the wall over the sofa. A badly framed landscape hung over one of the easy chairs. The inevitable television set stood in one corner of the room, and a window under which was a radiator occupied the other corner.

"Sit down, Bert," Bell said. "Molly!" he called again.

"Coming," a voice called from the other end of the house, an end he suspected was the kitchen.

"She's doing the dishes," Bell explained. "She'll be right in. Sit down, Bert." Kling sat in one of the easy chairs. Bell hovered over him, being the gracious host. "Can I get you something? A glass of beer? Cigar? Anything?"

"The last time I had a glass of beer," Kling said, "I got shot right afterwards."

"Well, ain't nobody going to shoot you here. Come on, have a glass. We've got some cold in the Frigidaire."

"No, thanks anyway," Kling said politely.

Molly Bell came into the room, drying her hands on a dish towel.

"You must be Bert," she said. "Peter's told me all about you." She gave her right hand a final wipe and then crossed to where Kling had stood up, and extended her hand. Kling took it, and she squeezed it warmly. In describing her, Bell had said, "Molly's no slouch—even now, pregnant and all." Kling hated to disagree, but he honestly found very little that was attractive in Molly Bell. She might at one time have been a knockout, but them days were gone forever. Even discounting the additional waist-high bulge of the expectant mother, Kling saw only a washed-out blonde with faded blue eyes. The eyes were very tired, and wrinkles radiated from their edges. Her hair had no luster; it hung from her head disconsolately. Her smile did not help, because it happened to be a radiant smile which served only as a contrast for the otherwise drab face. He was a little shocked, partly because of Bell's advance publicity, partly because he realized the girl couldn't have been much older than twenty-four or twenty-five.

"How do you do, Mrs. Bell?" he said.

"Oh, call me Molly. Please." There was something very warm about Molly, and he found himself liking her immensely, and somewhat disliking Bell for giving a build-up which couldn't fail to be disappointing. He wondered, too, if Jeannie was the "knockout" Bell had described. He had his doubts now.

"I'll get you a beer, Bert," Bell said.

"No, really, I—"

"Come on, come on," Bell said, overriding him and starting out toward the kitchen.

When he was gone, Molly said, "I'm so glad you could come, Bert. I think your talking to her will do a lot of good."

"Well, I'll try," Kling said. "Where is she?"

"In her room." Molly gestured with her head toward the other end of the house. "With the door locked." She shook her head. "That's what I mean. She behaves so strangely. I was seventeen once, Bert, and I didn't behave that way. She's a girl with troubles."

Kling nodded noncommittally.

Molly sat, her hands folded in her lap, her feet close

28

together. "I was a fun-loving girl when I was seven-teen," Molly said, somewhat wistfully. "You can ask Pe-ter. But Jeannie . . . I don't know. She's a girl with se-crets. Secrets, Bert." She shook her head again. "I try to be a sister and a mother both to her, but she won't tell me a thing. There's a wall between us, something that was never there before, and I can't understand it. Some-times I think—I think she hates me. Now why should she hate me? I've never done a thing to her, not a thing." Molly paused, sighing heavily.

"Well," Kling said diplomatically, "you know how kids are."

"Yes, I do," Molly said. "It hasn't been so long ago that I've forgotten. I'm only twenty-four, Bert. I know I look a lot older than that, but taking care of two kids can knock you out—and now another one coming, it isn't easy. And trying to handle Jeannie, too. It takes a lot out of a woman. But I was seventeen, too, and not so long ago, and I can remember. Jeannie isn't acting right. Something's troubling her, Bert. I read so much about teen-agers belonging to gangs and what not. I'm afraid. I think she may be in with a bad crowd, kids who are making her do bad things. That's what's troubling her, I think. I don't know. Maybe you can find out."

"Well, I'll certainly try."

"I'd appreciate it. I asked Peter to get a private detec-tive, but he said we couldn't afford it. He's right, of course. God knows, I can barely make ends meet with what he brings home." She sighed again. "But the big thing is Jeannie. If I can just find out what's *wrong* with her, what's made her the way she is now. She didn't used to be like this, Bert. It's only . . . I don't know . . . about a year ago now, I suppose. She sud-denly became a young lady, and just as suddenly she—she's slipped away from me."

Bell came back into the room, carrying a bottle of beer and a glass.

"Did you want one, honey?" he asked Molly.

"No, I've got to be careful." She turned to Kling. "The doctor says I'm putting on too much weight."

Bell poured the beer for Kling. He handed him the glass and said, "There's more in the bottle. I'll leave it here on the end table for you."

"Thank you," Kling said. He lifted his glass. "Well, here's to the new baby."

"Thank you," Molly said, smiling.

"Seems every time I turn around, Molly's pregnant again," Bell said. "It's fantastic."

"Oh, Peter," Molly said, still smiling.

"All I have to do is take a deep breath, and Molly's pregnant. She brought in a specimen of me to the hospital. The doctors told her I had enough there to fertilize the entire female population of China. How do you like that?"

"Well," Kling said, a little embarrassed.

"Oh, he's such a *man*," Molly said sarcastically. "It's me who has to carry them around, though."

"Did she tell you a little more about Jeannie?"

"Yes," Kling said.

"I'll get her for you in a few minutes." He looked at his watch. "I got to be taking the cab out soon, and I'll drop Molly off at a movie. Then you and Jeannie can talk alone—until our sitter gets here, anyway."

"You drive a lot at night?" Kling asked, making conversation.

"Three, four times a week. Depends on how good I do during the day. It's my own cab, and I'm my own boss."

"I see," Kling said. He sipped at the beer. It was not as cold as Bell had advertised it. He began to doubt seriously *any* of Bell's advance promotion, and he looked forward to meeting Jeannie with vague skepticism.

"I'll get her," Bell said.

Kling nodded. Molly tensed where she sat on the edge of the sofa. Bell left the room and walked through the apartment. Kling heard him knocking on the closed door, and then heard his voice saying, "Jeannie? Jeannie?"

There was a muffled answer which Kling could not decipher; then Bell said, "There's a friend of mine I'd like you to meet. Nice young feller. Come on out, won't you?"

There was another muffled answer, and then Kling heard a lock being unsnapped and a door opening and a young girl's voice asking, "Who is he?"

"Friend of mine," Bell said. "Come on, Jeannie."

Kling heard footsteps coming through the apartment.

He busied himself with the glass of beer. When he lifted his head, Bell was standing in the doorway to the room, the girl beside him—and Kling no longer doubted his veracity.

The girl was a little taller than Molly. She wore her blond hair clipped close to her head, and it was the blondest hair Kling had ever seen in his life. It was almost yellow, like ripe corn, and he knew instantly that she had never touched it. The hair was as natural as her face, and her face was a perfect oval with a slightly tilted nose and wide, clear blue eyes. Her brows were black, as if fate hadn't been able to make up its mind, and they arched over the blue eyes, suspended between them and the yellow hair, strikingly beautiful. Her lips were full, and she wore a pale-orange lipstick, and her mouth was not smiling.

She wore a straight black skirt and a blue sweater, the sleeves shoved up to her elbows. She was a slender girl, but a slender girl with the remarkable combination of good hips and firm, full breasts that crowded her sweater. Her legs were good, too. Her thighs were full, and her calves were beautifully curved, and even the loafers she wore could not hide the natural splendor of her legs.

She was a woman, and a beautiful woman.

Peter Bell hadn't lied. His sister-in-law was a knockout.

"Jeannie, this is Bert Kling. Bert, I'd like you to meet my sister-in-law, Jeannie Paige."

Kling got to his feet. "How do you do?" he said.

"Hi," Jeannie answered. She did not move from where she stood alongside Bell.

"Bert's a cop," Bell said. "Maybe you read about him. He got shot in a bar downtown."

"*Outside* the bar," Kling corrected.

"Sure, well," Bell said. "Honey, your sister and I have to go now, and Bert only just got here, so I thought you wouldn't mind talking to him a while—until the sitter gets here, huh?"

"Where are you going?" Jeannie asked.

"I got to hack a while, and Molly's taking in a movie."

"Oh," Jeannie said, looking at Kling suspiciously. "So okay?" Bell asked.

31

"Sure," Jeannie replied.

"I'll take off this apron and comb my hair," Molly said. Kling watched her as she rose. He could see the resemblance between her and Jeannie now, and he could now believe that Molly, too, had been a damned attractive woman once. But marriage and motherhood, and work and worry, had taken a great deal out of her. She was no match now for her younger sister, if she had ever been. She went out of the living room and into a room Kling supposed was the bathroom.

"It's a nice night," Kling said awkwardly.

"Is it?" Jeannie asked.

"Yes."

"Molly! Hurry up!" Bell called.

"Coming," she answered from the bathroom.

"Very mild. For autumn, I mean," Kling said. Jeannie made no comment.

In a few minutes, Molly came out of the bathroom, her hair combed, fresh lipstick on her mouth. She put on her coat and said, "If you go out, don't come home too late, Jeannie."

"Don't worry," Jeannie answered.

"Well, good night. It was nice meeting you, Bert. Call us, won't you?"

"Yes, I will."

Bell paused with his hand on the doorknob. "I'm leaving her in your hands, Bert," he said. "Good night." He and Molly went out of the room, closing the door behind them. Kling heard the outside door slam shut. The room was dead silent. Outside, he heard a car starting. He assumed it was Bell's cab.

"Whose idea was this?" Jeannie asked.

"I don't understand," Kling said.

"Your coming here. Hers?"

"No. Peter's an old friend of mine."

"Yeah?"

"Yes."

"How old are you?" Jeannie asked.

"Twenty-four," Kling said.

"Is she trying to fix us up or something?"

"What?"

"Molly. Is she trying to finagle something?"

"I don't know what you mean."

Jeannie stared at him levelly. Her eyes were very blue. He watched her face, suddenly overwhelmed by her beauty. "You're not as dumb as you sound, are you?" she asked.

"I'm not trying to sound dumb," Kling said.

"I'm asking you whether or not Molly has plans for you and me."

Kling smiled. "No, I don't think she has."

"I wouldn't put it past her," Jeannie said.

"I take it you don't like your sister very much."

Jeannie seemed suddenly alert. "She's okay," she answered.

"But?"

"No buts. My sister is fine."

"Then why do you resent her?"

"Because I know Peter wouldn't go hollering cop, so this must be her idea."

"I'm here as a friend, not as a cop."

"Yeah, I'll bet," Jeannie said. "You'd better drink your beer. I'm leaving as soon as that sitter arrives."

"Got a date?" Kling asked casually.

"Who wants to know?"

"I do."

"It's none of your business."

"That puts me in my place, I guess."

"It should," Jeannie said.

"You seem a lot older than seventeen."

For a moment, Jeannie bit her lip. "I *am* a lot older than seventeen," she answered then. "A whole lot older, Mr. Kling."

"Bert," he corrected. "What's the matter, Jeannie? You haven't smiled once since I met you."

"Nothing's the matter."

"Trouble at school?"

"No."

"Boy-friend?"

She hesitated. "No."

"Ah-ha," Kling said. "When you're seventeen, it's usually a boy-friend."

"I haven't got a boy-friend."

"No. What then? Crush on someone who doesn't care?"

33

"Stop it!" Jeannie said harshly. "This is none of your business. You've no right to pry!"

"I'm sorry," Kling said. "I was trying to help. You're not in any kind of trouble, are you?"

"No."

"I meant with the law."

"No. And if I was, I certainly wouldn't tell it to a cop."

"I'm a friend, remember?"

"Sure, friend."

"You're a very pretty girl, Jeannie."

"So I've been told."

"A pretty girl can find herself in with the wrong crowd. A pretty girl—"

"— is like a melody," Jeannie concluded. "I'm *not* in with the wrong crowd. I'm fine. I'm a healthy, normal teen-ager. Leave me alone."

"Do you date much?"

"Enough."

"Anyone steady?"

"No."

"Anyone in mind for a steady?"

"Do *you* date much?" Jeannie countered.

"Not much."

"Anyone steady?"

"No," Kling answered, smiling.

"Anyone in mind for a steady?"

"No."

"Why not? I should think a hero cop would be in wild demand."

"I'm shy," Kling said.

"I'll just bet you are. We haven't known each other ten minutes, and we're discussing my love life. What'll you ask next? My brassière size?" Kling's eyes dropped inadvertently to the sweater. "I'll save you the trouble," Jeannie snapped. "It's a thirty-eight, C-cut."

"I figured as much," Kling answered.

"That's right, I keep forgetting you're a cop. Cops are very observant, aren't they? Are you the force's prize detective?"

"I'm a patrolman," Kling said levelly.

"Smart fellow like you, only a patrolman?"

34

"What the hell's eating you?" Kling asked suddenly, his voice rising.

"Nothing. What's eating you?"

"I never met a kid like you. You've got a decent home, you've got looks any other girl would chop off her right arm for, and you sound—"

"I'm the belle of Riverhead, didn't you know? I've got boys crying for—"

"—and you sound as if you're sixty years old living in a tenement flat! What the hell's eating you, girl?"

"Nothing. I simply don't like the idea of a cop coming around to ask me questions."

"Your people felt you needed help," Kling said wearily. "I don't know why. Seems to me you could step into a cage of tigers and come out unscratched. You're about as soft as an uncut diamond."

"Thanks."

Kling rose. "Take care of your beauty, kid," he said. "You may not have it when you're thirty-five." He started for the door.

"Bert," she called.

He turned. She was staring at the floor. "I'm sorry," she said. "I'm not usually a bitch."

"What is it?" he asked.

"Nothing, really. I have to work it out for myself, that's all." She smiled tremulously. "Everything'll be all right."

"Okay, he said. "Don't let it kill you. Everybody's got troubles. Especially at seventeen."

"I know," she said, still smiling.

"Listen, can I buy you an ice cream or something? Take your mind off your troubles."

"No, thanks," she said. She looked at her watch. "I have an appointment."

"Oh. Well, okay. Have fun, Jeannie.." He looked at her closely. "You're a beautiful girl. You should be enjoying yourself."

"I know," she answered.

"If you should need anything—if you should feel I can help—you can call me at the 87th Precinct." He smiled. "That's where I work."

"All right. Thanks."

"Want to walk down with me?"

35

"No, I have to wait for the sitter."

Kling snapped his fingers. "Sure." He paused. "If you'd like me to wait with you . . ."

"I'd rather you didn't. Thanks, anyway."

"Okay," Kling said. He looked at her once more. Her face was troubled, very troubled. He knew there was more to say, but he didn't know how to say it. "Take care of yourself," he managed.

"I will. Thanks."

"Sure," Kling said. He opened the door and stepped into the foyer. Behind him, Jeannie Paige locked the door.

5

Willis did not like working overtime. There are very few people who enjoy working overtime, unless they are paid for it. Willis was a detective/3rd grade and his salary was $5,230 a year. He was not paid by the hour, nor was he paid by the number of crimes he solved yearly. His salary was $5,230, and that was what he got no matter how many hours he put in.

He was somewhat miffed, therefore, when Fats Donner failed to call him that Wednesday night. He had hung around the Squad Room, answering the phone every time it rang, and generally making a nuisance of himself with the bulls who had come in on relief. He had listened for a while to Meyer, who was telling Temple about some case the 33rd had, where some guy was going around stealing cats. The story had not interested him, and he had continually glanced at the big clock on the wall, waiting. He left the house at nine, convinced that Donner would not call that night.

When he reported for work at seven-forty-five the next morning, the desk sergeant handed him a note which told him Donner had called at eleven-fifteen the night before. Donner had asked that Willis call him back as soon as possible. A number was listed on the sheet of paper. Willis walked past the desk and to the right, where a rectangular sign and a pointing hand showed the way to the DETECTIVE DIVISION. He climbed the metal steps, turned where the grilled window threw a pale grayish morning light on a five-by-five-square interruption of the steps, and then proceeded up another sixteen steps to the second floor.

He turned his back to the doors at the end of the corridor, the doors marked LOCKERS. He walked past the benches and the MEN'S LAVATORY, and the CLERICAL office, and then through the slatted rail divider and into the Detective Squad Room. He signed in, said Good morning to Havilland and Simpson, who were having coffee at one of the desks, and then went to his own desk and slid the phone toward him. It was a gray, dull morning, and the hanging light globes cast a dust-covered luminescence over the room. He dialed the number and waited, looking over toward Byrnes' office. The lieutenant's door was wide open, which meant the lieutenant had not arrived. Byrnes generally closed his door as soon as he was in his office.

"Got a hot lead, Hal?" Havilland called.

"Yeah," Willis said. A voice on the other end of his phone said, "Hello?" The voice was sleepy, but he recognized it as Donner's.

"Fats, this is Willis. You called me last night?"

"What?" Donner said.

"Detective Willis, 87th Squad," Willis aid.

"Oh. Hi. Man, what time is it?"

"About eight."

"Don't you cats never sleep?"

"What've you got for me?"

"You make a stud going by Skippy Randolph?"

"Not off the bat. Who is he?"

"He's recently from Chi, but I'm pretty sure he's got a record here, too. He's been mugging."

"You sure?"

"Straight goods. You want to meet him?"

"Maybe."

"There's gonna be a little cube rolling tonight. Randolph'll be there. You can rub elbows."

"Where?"

"I'll take you," Donner said. He paused. "Steam baths cost, you know."

"Let me check him out first," Willis said. "He may

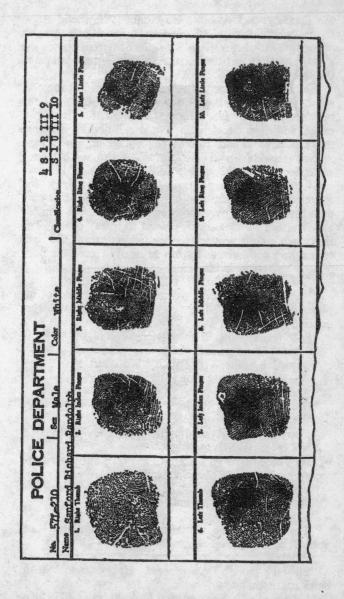

POLICE DEPARTMENT

No. 577-210 | Sex Male | Color White | Classification $\frac{4\ 8\ 1\ R\ III\ 9}{S\ 1\ U\ III\ 10}$

Name Sanford Richard Randolph

1. Right Thumb	2. Right Index Finger	3. Right Middle Finger	4. Right Ring Finger	5. Right Little Finger
6. Left Thumb	7. Left Index Finger	8. Left Middle Finger	9. Left Ring Finger	10. Left Little Finger

38

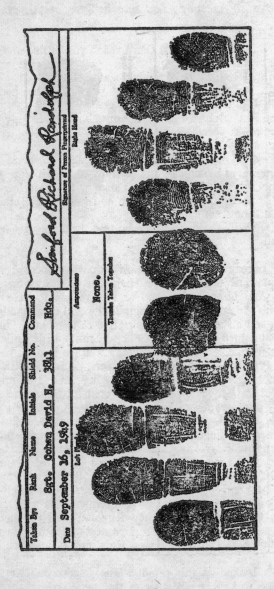

Taken By   Rank   Name   Initials   Shield No.   Command

Sgt.   Cohen David H., 3813   Hdq.

Date September 16, 1949

Signature of Person Fingerprinted

Sanford Richard Randolph

Amputations

None.

Left Thumb Taken Regular

Thumbs Taken Regular

Right Hand

39

not be worth meeting. You sure he'll be at this crap game?"

"Posilutely, dad."

"I'll call you back later. Can I reach you at this number?"

"Until eleven. I'll be at the baths after that."

Willis looked at the name he'd written on his pad. "Skippy Randolph. His own moniker?"

"The Randolph is. I'm not so sure about the Skippy."

"But you're sure he's mugging?"

"Absotively," Donner said.

"Okay, I'll call you back." Willis replaced the reciever, thought for a moment, and then dialed the Bureau of Criminal Identification. Miscolo, one of the patrolmen from Clerical came into the office and said, "Hey, Hal, you want some coffee?

"Yes," Willis said, and then he told the I.B. what he wanted.

The bureau of Criminal Identification was located at Headquarters, downtown on High Street. It was open twenty-four hours a day, and its sole reason for existence was the collection and compilation and cataloguing of any and all information descriptive of criminals. The I.B. maintained a Fingerprint File, a Criminal Idex File, a Wanted File, a Degenerate File, a Parolee File, a Released Prisoner File, a Known Gamblers, Known Rapists, Known Muggers, Known Any-and-All Kinds of Criminal Files. Its Modus Operandi File contained more than 80,000 photographs of known criminals. And since all persons charged with and convicted of a crime are photographed and fingerprinted as specified by law, the file was continually growing and continually being brought up to date. Since I.B. recieved and classified some 206,000 sets of prints yearly, and since it answered requests for some 250,000 criminal records from departments all over the country, Willis' request was a fairly simple one to answer, and they delivered their package to him within the hour. The first photostated item Willis dug out of the envelope was Randolph's fingerprint card.

Willis looked at this rapidly. The fingerprints were worthless to him at this stage of the game. He reached

40

into the envelope and pulled out the next item, a photostated copy of the back of Randolph's fingerprint card.

Willis looked through the other items in the envelope. There was a card stating that Randolph had been released from Baily's after eight months of good behavior on May 2, 1950. He had notified his parole officer that he wished to return to Chicago, the city in which he was born, the city he should have returned to as soon as he'd been discharged from the Marine Corps. Permission had been granted, and he'd left the city for Chicago on June 5, 1950. There was a written report from the Chicago parole office to which Randolph's records had been transferred. Apparently, he had in no way violated his parole.

IDENTIFICATION BUREAU

Name Sanford Richard Randolph

Identification Jacket Number M381904

Alias "Skippy" "Skip" "Skipper" "Scuppers" Randolph
Color White

Residence 29 Hunter Lane, Calm's Point

Date of Birth January 12, 1918   Age 31

Birthplace Chicago, Illinois

Height 5' 10"   Weight 163   Hair Brown   Eyes Blue

Comp. Fair   Occupation Truck driver

Scars and Tattoos Knife scar on left temple, half inch in length. Tattoo on right biceps, "Mother" in heart. Tattoo on right forearm, Anchor. Tattoo on left forearm, Marine Corps Shield and "Semper Fidelis." Bullet-wound scar, left leg.

Arrested By Det. 2nd/Gr. Peter Di Labbio

Detective Division Number 37-1046-1949

Date of Arrest 9/15/49   Place South 74 Street, Isola

Charge Assault with intent to commit a felony

Brief Details of Crime Randolph attacked a 53-year-old man, beat him, and then demanded his wallet. Det. Di Labbio, cruising in area, apprehended him as he held victim against wall of building.

Previous Record None

Indicted Criminal Courts, September 16, 1949

Final Charge Assault in second degree, Penal Law 242

Disposition One year's imprisonment in workhouse at Baily's Island.

41

Willis thumbed through the material and came up with a transcript of Randolph's Marine Corps record. He had enlisted on December 8, the day after Pearl Harbor. He was twenty-three years old at the time, almost twenty-four. He had risen to the rank of corporal, had taken part in the landings at Iwo Jima and Okinawa and had personally been responsible for the untimely demise of fifty-four Japanese soldiers. On June 17, 1945, he was wounded in the leg during a Sixth Marine Division attack against the town of Mezado. He had been sent back for hospitalization on Pearl, and after convalescence he was sent to San Francisco, where he was honorably discharged.

And four years later, he mugged a fifty-three-year-old man and tried to take his wallet.

And now according to Donner, he was back in the city—and mugging again.

Willis looked at his watch, and then dialed Donner's number.

"Hello?" Donner asked.

"This crap game tonight," Willis said. "Set it up."

The crap game in question was of the floating variety, and on this particular Thursday night it was being held in a warehouse close to the River Highway. Willis, in keeping with the festive spirit of the occasion, wore a sport shirt patterned with horses' heads and a sport jacket. When he met Donner, he almost didn't recognize him. Somehow, the flabby quivering pile of white flesh that sucked in steam at the Turkish baths managed to acquire stature and even eminence when it was dumped into a dark-blue suit. Donner still looked immense, but immense now like a legendary giant, magnificent, almost regal in his bearing. He shook hands with Willis, during which ceremony a ten-dollar bill passed from one palm to another, and then they headed for the warehouse, the crap game, and Skippy Randolph.

A skinny man at the side door recognized Donner, but took pause until Donner introduced Hal Willis as "Willy Harris, an old chum." He passed them into the warehouse then, the first floor of which was dark except for a light bulb hanging in one corner of the room. The crapshooters were huddled under that bulb. The rest of the room was crowded with what seemed to be mostly refrigerators and ranges.

"There's a fix in with the watchman and the cop on the beat," Donner explained "Won't anybody bother us here." They walked across the room, their heels sounding noisily on the concrete floor. "Randolph is the one in the green jacket," Donner said. "You want me to introduce you, or will you make it alone?"

"Alone is better," Willis said. "If this gets fouled, I don't want it going back to you. You're valuable."

"The harm's already done," Donner said. "I passed you through the door, didn't I?"

"Sure, but I *could* be a smart cop who even had you fooled."

"Gone," Donner said. And then—in a whisper, so that his heartfelt compliment would not sound like apple-polishing—he added, "You *are* a smart cop."

If Willis heard him, he gave no sign of it. They walked over to where the blanket was spread beneath the light bulb. Donner crowded into the circle of bettors, and Willis moved into the circle opposite him, standing alongside Randolph. A short man with a turtle-neck sweater was rolling.

"What's his point?" Willis asked Randolph.

Randolph looked down at Willis. He was a tall man with brown hair and blue eyes. The knife scar on his temple gave his otherwise pleasant face a menacing look. "Six," he said.

"He hot?"

"Luke," Randolph replied.

The man in the turtle-neck sweater picked up the cubes and rolled again.

"Come on six," someone across the circle said.

"Stop praying," another man warned. Willis counted heads. Including himself and Donner, there were seven men in the game. The dice rolled to a stop.

"Six," the man in the turtle-neck sweater said. He picked up most of the bills on the blanket, leaving twenty-five dollars. He retrieved the dice then and said, "Bet twenty-five."

"You're covered," a big man with a gravelly voice said. He dropped two tens and a five onto the blanket. The man in the turtle neck rolled.

"Come seven," he said.

Willis watched. The dice bounced, then stopped moving.

"Little Joe," the turtle neck said.

"Two-to-one no four," Willis said. He held out a ten-spot.

A man across the circle said, "Got you," and handed him a five. Turtle Neck rolled again.

"That's a crazy bet," Randolph whispered to Willis.

"You said he was luke."

"He's getting warmer every time he rolls. Watch him."

Turtle Neck rolled a six, and then, a five. The man across the circle said to Willis, "Take another five on that?"

"It's a bet, Willis said. He palmed a ten, and the man covered it with a five. Turtle Neck rolled. He got his four on the next throw. Willis handed the thirty dollars to the man across the circle. Turtle Neck left the fifty on the blanket.

"I'll take half of it, Gravel said.

"I've got the other half," Willis said.

They dropped their money, covering Turtle Neck's.

"You're nuts," Randolph said.

"I came here to bet," Willis answered. "When I want to knit argyles, I'll stay home."

Turtle Neck rolled a seven on his first throw.

"Son of a bitch!" Gravel said.

"Leave the hundred," Turtle Neck replied, smiling.

"You're covered," Willis told him. From across the circle, Donner eyed Willis dubiously. Gravel's eyebrows went up onto his forehead.

"We've got a sport with us," Turtle Neck said.

"Is this a sewing circle or a crap game?" Willis asked. "Shoot."

Turtle Neck rolled an eight.

"Six-to-five no eight," Willis said. The men in the circle were silent. "All right, eight-to-five." Six-to-five was the proper bet.

"Bet," Gravel said, handing Willis a fiver.

"Roll," Willis said.

Turtle Neck rolled.

"Box cars," Randolph said. He looked at Willis for a

44

moment. "I've got another eight bucks says no eight," he said.

"Same bet?" Gravel asked.

"Same."

"You're on." He handed Randolph his five.

"I thought this guy was getting hot," Willis said, smiling at Randolph.

"What gets hot, gets cool," Randolph replied.

Turtle Neck rolled his eight. Gravel collected from Willis and Randolph. A hook-nosed man across the circle sighed.

"Bet the two hundred," Turtle Neck said.

"This is getting kind of steep, ain't it? Hook Nose asked.

"If it's too steep for you, go home to bed," Randolph answered.

"Who's taking the two hundred?" Turtle Neck asked.

"I'll take fifty of it," Hook Nose said, sighing.

"That leaves a C and a half," Turtle Neck said. "Am I covered?"

"Here's a century," Willis said. He dropped a bill onto the blanket.

"I'll take the last fifty," Randolph said, throwing his money down with Willis'. "Roll, hot-shot."

"These are big-timers," a round-faced man standing on Willis' right said. "Big gamblers."

Turtle Neck rolled. The cubes bounced across the blanket. One die stopped, showing a deuce. The second die clicked against it and abruptly stopped with a five face up.

"Seven," Turtle Neck said, smiling.

"He's hot," Round Face said.

"Too damn hot," Hook Nose mumbled.

"Bet," Gravel put in.

"Bet the four hundred."

"Come on," Hook Nose said. "You trying to drive us home?"

Willis looked across the circle. Hook Nose was carrying a gun, its outline plainly etched against his jacket. And, if he was not mistaken, both Turtle Neck and Gravel were heeled, too.

"I'll take two bills of it," Willis said.

45

"Anybody covering the other two? Turtle Neck asked.

"You got to cool off sometime," Randolph said. "You got a bet." He dropped two hundred onto the blanket.

"Roll 'em," Willis said. "Shake 'em first."

"Papa's shoes got holes, dice," Turtle Neck said, and he rolled an eleven.

"Man, I'm hot tonight. Bet it all," he said. "Am I covered?"

"Slow down a little, cousin," Willis said suddenly.

"I'm betting the eight," Turtle Neck answered.

"Let's see the ivories," Willis said.

"What!"

"I said let me see the cubes. They act talented."

"The talent's in the fist, friend," Turtle Neck said. "You covering me or not?"

"Not until I see the dice."

"Then you ain't covering me." Turtle Neck answered dryly. "Who's betting?"

"Show him the dice," Randolph said. Willis watched him. The ex-Marine had lost two bills on that last roll. Willis had intimated that the dice were crooked, and now Randolph wanted to see for himself.

"These dice are straight," Turtle Neck said.

Gravel stared at Willis peculiarly. "They're Honest Johns, stranger," he put in. "We run a square game."

"They act drunk," Willis said. "Prove it to me."

"You don't like the game, you can cut out," Hook Nose said.

"I've dropped half a G since I walked in," Willis snapped. "I practically own those dice. Do I get a look or don't I?"

"You bring this guy in, Fats?" Gravel asked.

"Yeah," Donner said. He was beginning to sweat. "Where'd you dig him up?"

"We met in a bar," Willis said, automatically clearing Donner. "I told him I was looking for action. I didn't expect educated dice."

"We told you the dice are square," Gravel said.

"Then give me a look."

"You can study them when they're passed to you," Turtle Neck said. "It's still my roll."

46

"Nobody rolls till I see them dice," Willis snapped.

"For a small man, you talk a big game," Gravel said.

"Try me," Willis said softly.

Gravel looked him over, apparently trying to determine whether or not Willis was heeled. Deciding that he wasn't, he said, "Get out of here, you scrawny punk. I'd snap you in two."

"Try me, you big tub of crap!" Willis shouted.

Gravel stared hotly at Willis for an instant, and then made the same mistake countless men before him had made. There was, you see, no way of telling from Willis' appearance what his training had been. There was no way of knowing that he was expert in the ways of judo, or that he could practically break your back by snapping his fingers. Gravel simply assumed he was a scrawny punk, and he rushed across the circle, ready to squash Willis like a bug.

He was, to indulge in complete understatement, somewhat surprised by what happened to him next.

Willis didn't watch Gravel's face or Gravel's hands. He watched his feet, timing himself to rush forward when Gravel's right foot was in a forward position. He did that suddenly, and then dropped to his right knee and grabbed Gravel's left ankle.

"Hey, what the hell—" Gravel started, but that was all he ever said. Willis pulled the ankle toward him and upward off the ground. In the same instant, he shoved out at Gravel's gut with the heel of his right hand. Gravel, seeing his opponent drop to his knees, feeling the fingers tight around his ankle, feeling the sharp thrust at his mid-section, didn't know he was experiencing an Ankle Throw. He only knew that he was suddenly falling backward, and then he felt the wind rush out of him as his back collided with the concrete floor. He shook his head, bellowed, and jumped to his feet.

Willis was standing opposite him, grinning.

"Okay, smart guy," Gravel said. "Okay, you smart little bastard," and he rushed forward again.

Willis didn't move a muscle. He stood balanced evenly, smiling, waiting, and then he struck suddenly.

He grabbed Gravel's left arm at the elbow bend, cupping it with his right hand. Without hesitation, he snapped Gravel's left arm upward and forced his left

47

hand into Gravel's armpit. His hand was opened flat, but the fingers were not spread. They lay close together, the thumb tucked under them, out of the way. Willis wheeled to the right, swinging Gravel's arm over his left shoulder and forcing it downward by pressing on the elbow grip.

He bent forward suddenly, and Gravel's feet left the ground, and then Willis gave a sharp jerk and Gravel found himself spinning upward in a Shoulder Overthrow, the concrete coming up to meet him.

Considerately, and because he didn't want to break Gravel's arm, Willis released his grip on the elbow before Gravel smashed into the concrete. Gravel shook his head, dazed. He tried to get up, and then he sat down again, still shaking his head. Across the circle, Hook Nose's hand snaked toward the opening of his jacket.

"Hold it right there!" a voice said.

Willis turned. Randolph was holding a .45 in his fist, covering the others. "Thanks," Willis said.

"Scoop up that eight hundred," Randolph answered. "I don't like crooked games."

"Hey, that's my dough!" Turtle Neck shouted.

"It used to be ours," Randolph replied.

Willis picked up the money and put it in his pocket. "Come on," Randolph said. They started for the side door, Randolph backing away from the circle, still holding the .45. The skinny man who'd passed Willis in looked confused, but he didn't say anything. Most men don't when a .45 is in the picture. Willis and Randolph ran down the street. Randolph pocketed the gun, and hailed a cab on the corner.

"You like a cup of coffee?" Randolph asked.

"Sure," Willis said.

Randolph extended his hand. "My name's Skippy Randolph."

Willis took it. "Mine's Willy Harris."

"Where'd you learn judo?" Randolph asked.

"In the Marines," Willis said.

"It figured. I was in the corps, too."

"No kidding?" Willis said, feigning surprise.

"Sixth Division," Randolph said proudly.

"I was in the Third," Willis said.

"Iwo?"

"Yes," Willis said.

"I was in Iwo and Okinawa both. My company was attached with the Fifth when we hit Iwo."

"That was a goddamn mess," Willis said.

"You said it. Still, I had some good times with the corps. Caught a slug at Okinawa, though."

"I was lucky," Willis said. He looked around for wood to knock, and then rapped his knuckles on his head.

"You think we're far enough away from those creeps?" Randolph asked.

"I think so."

"Any place here," Randolph told the cabbie. The driver pulled up to the curb, and Randolph tipped him. They stood on the sidewalk, and Randolph looked up the street. "There's a coffeepot," he said, pointing.

Willis took the eight hundred dollars from his pocket. "Half of this is yours," he said. He handed Randolph the bills.

"I figured them dice were a little too peppy," Randolph said, taking the money.

"Yeah," Willis said dryly. They opened the door to the coffeepot and walked to a table in the corner. They ordered coffee and French crullers. When the order came, they sat quietly for a while.

"Good coffee," Randolph said.

"Yeah," Willis agreed.

"You a native in this burg?"

"Yeah. You?"

"Chicago, originally," Randolph said. "I drifted here when I was discharged. Stuck around for four years."

"When were you discharged?"

"Forty-five," Randolph said. "Went back to Chicago in fifty."

"What happened to forty-nine?"

"I did some time," Randolph said, watching Willis warily.

"Haven't we all?" Willis said evenly. "What'd they get you on?"

"I mugged an old duffer."

"What brings you back here?" Willis asked.

"What'd they get *you* for ?" Randolph asked.

"Oh, nothing," Willis said.

49

"No, come on."

"What difference does it make?"

"I'm curious," Randolph said.

"Rape," Willis said quickly.

"Hey," Randolph said, raising his brows.

"It ain't like what it sounds. I was going with this dame, and she was the biggest tease alive. So one night—"

"Sure, I understand."

"Do you?" Willis said levelly.

"Sure. You think I wanted to mug that old crumb? I just needed dough, that's all."

"What're you doing for cash now?" Willis asked.

"I been makin' out."

"Doing what?"

Randolph hesitated. "I'm a truck driver."

"Yeah?"

"Yeah."

"Who do you work for?"

"Well, I ain't workin' at it right now."

"What *are* you working at?"

"I got something going, brings in a little steady cash." He paused. "You looking for something?"

"I might be."

"Two guys could really make out."

"Doing what?"

"You figure it," Randolph said.

"I don't like playing 'What's My Line?'," Willis answered. "If you've got something for me, let me hear it."

"Mugging," Randolph said.

"Old guys?"

"Old guys, young guys, what's the diff?"

"There ain't much dough in mugging."

"In the right neighborhoods, there is."

"I don't know," Willis said. "I don't like the idea of knocking over old guys." He paused. "And dames."

"Who said anything about dames? I steer away from them. You get all kinds of trouble with dames."

"Yeah?" Willis said.

"Sure. Well, Jesus, don't *you* know? They get you on attempted rape as well as assualt. Even if you didn't lay a hand on the bitch."

"That right?" Willis said, somewhat disappointed.

50

"Sure. I stay away like they're poison. Besides, most dames don't carry too much cash."

"I see," Willis said.

"So what do you think? You know judo and I know it, too. We could knock this city on its ass."

"I don't know," Willis said, convinced that Randolph was not his man now, but wanting to hear more so that he could set him up for a pinch. "Tell me more about how you work it."

While the two men talked in one part of the city, the girl lay face down in the bushes in another part of the city.

The bushes were at the base of a sharp incline, a miniature cliff of earth and stone. The cliff sloped down toward the bushes, and beyond the bushes was the River, and arching overhead was the long span of the bridge leading to the next state.

The girl lay in a crooked heap.

Her stockings had been torn when she rolled down the incline to the bushes, and her skirt was twisted so that the backs of her legs were exposed clear to her buttocks. The legs were good legs, youthful legs, but one was twisted at a curious angle, and there was nothing attractive about the girl's body as it lay in the bushes.

The girl's face was bleeding. The blood spread from the broken features to the stiff branches of the bushes and then to the ground, where the parched autumn earth drank it up thirstily. One arm was folded across the girl's full breasts, pressed against the sharp, cutting twigs of the bushes. The other arm dangled loosely at her side. Her hand was open.

On the ground, close to the spreading blood, several feet from the girl's open palm, a pair of sunglasses rested. One of the lenses in the glasses was shattered.

The girl had blond hair, but the bright yellow was stained with blood where something hard and unyielding had repeatedly smashed at her skull.

The girl was not breathing. She lay face down in the bushes at the bottom of the small cliff, her blood rushing onto the ground, and she would never breathe again.

The girl's name was Jeannie Paige.

6

Lieutenant Byrnes studied the information on the printed sheet.

POLICE DEPARTMENT

Date: September 15

From: Commanding Officer, Lt. Peter Byrnes, 87th Pct.

To: Chief Medical Examiner

SUBJECT: DEATH OF Jeanne Rita Paige

Please furnish information on items checked below in connection with the death of the above named. Body was found on September 14 at foot of Hamilton Bridge, Isola.

Autopsy performed or examination made? Preliminary

By Dr. Bertram Nelson, Asst. Medical Examiner, St. Joan's Hosp.

Date: September 14   Where? County Mortuary

Cause of death: Brain concussion apparently. (Note: only cursory examination made before your request for information.)

Result of chemical analysis: Not performed as yet.

Body identified to Medical Examiner by: Mrs. Peter Bell

Address: 412 De Witt Street, Riverhead

Relationship: Sister

Body claimed by: (name and address):

If not claimed, disposition of same: Body is at mortuary. Complete autopsy is now being undertaken. Mrs. Bell has indicated she will claim body upon completion of tests. Full necropsy report will follow.

Burial Permit No.

Other information desired:

Arthur N. Burgher MD

OFFICE OF CHIEF MEDICAL EXAMINER

Translated into English, it simply meant that somebody had goofed. The body had been taken to the mortuary, and some half-assed intern there had probably very carefully studied the broken face and the shattered skull and come up with the remarkable conclusion that death had been caused by "brain concussion apparently." He could understand why a full report was not on his desk, but even understanding, the knowledge griped him. He could not expect people, he supposed, to go gallivanting around in the middle of the night—the body had probably been delivered to the mortuary in the wee hours—trying to discover whether or not a stomach holds poison. No, of course not. Nobody starts work until nine in the morning, and nobody works after five in the afternoon. A wonderful country. Short hours for everyone.

Except the fellow who killed this girl, of course.

He hadn't minded a little overtime, not him.

Seventeen years old, Byrnes thought. *Jesus, my son is seventeen!*

He walked to the door of his office. He was a short, solidly packed man with a head that seemed to have been blasted loose from a huge chunk of granite. He had small blue eyes which constantly darted, perpetually alert. He didn't like people getting killed. He didn't like young girls getting their heads smashed in. He opened the door.

"Hal!" he called.

Willis looked up from his desk.

"Come in here, will you?" He left the door and began pacing the office. Willis came into the room and stood quietly, his hands behind his back.

"Anything on those sunglasses yet?" Byrnes asked, still pacing.

"No, sir. There was a good thumbprint on the unbroken lens, but it's not likely we'll get a make on a single print."

"What about your pal? The one you brought in last night?"

"Randolph. He's mad as hell because I conned him into making a full confession to a cop. I think he suspects it won't stand up in court, though. He's screaming for a lawyer right now."

"I'm talking about the thumbprint."

"It doesn't match up with his, sir," Willis said.

"Think it's the girl's?"

"No, sir, it isn't. We've already checked that."

53

"Then Randolph isn't our man."

"No, sir."

"I didn't think he was, anyway. This girl was probably knocked over while Randolph was with you."

"Yes, sir."

"It's a goddamn shame," Byrnes said, "a goddamn shame." He began pacing again. "What's Homicide North doing?"

"They're on it, sir. Rounding up all sex offenders."

"We can give them a hand with that. Check our files and put the boys to work, will you?" He paused. "You think our mugger did this?"

"The sunglasses might indicate that, sir."

"So Clifford's finally crossed the line, the bastard."

"It's a possibility, sir."

"My name is Pete," Byrnes said. "Why the formality?"

"Well, sir, I had an idea."

"About this thing?"

"Yes, sir. If our mugger did it, sir."

"Pete!" Byrnes roared.

"Pete, this son of a btich is terrorzing the city. Did you see the papers this morning? A seventeen-year-old kid, her face beaten to a bloody pulp! In our precinct, Pete. Okay, it's a rotten precinct. It stinks to high heaven, and there are people who think it'll always stink. But it burns me up, Pete. Jesus, it makes me sore."

"This precinct isn't so bad," Byrne said reflectively.

"Ah, Pete," Willis said, sighing.

"All right, it smells. We're doing our best. What the hell do they expect here? Snob Hill?"

"No. But we've got to give them protection, Pete."

"We are, aren't we? Three hundred and sixty-five days a year, every goddamn year. It's only the big things that make the papers. This goddamn mugger—"

"That's why we have to get him. Homicide North'll dicker around with this thing forever. Another body. All Homicide cops *see* is bodies. You think another one's going to get them in an uproar?"

"They do a good job," Byrnes said.

"I know, I know," Willis said impatiently. "But I think my idea'll help them."

"Okay," Byrnes said, "let's hear it."

The living room on that Friday afternoon was silent with the pallor of death. Molly Bell had done all her crying, and there were no more tears inside her, and so she sat silently, and her husband sat opposite her, and Bert Kling stood uneasily by the door, wondering why he had come.

He could clearly remember the girl Jeannie when she'd called him back as he was leaving Wednesday night. Incredible beauty, and etched beneath the beauty the clutching claws of trouble and worry. And now she was dead. And, oddly, he felt somehow responsible.

"Did she say anything to you?" Bell asked.

"Not much," Kling replied. "She seemed troubled about something . . . second . . . very cynical and bitter for a kid her age. I don't know." He shook his head.

"I knew there was something wrong," Molly said. Her voice was very low, barely audible. She clutched a handkerchief in her lap, but the handkerchief was dry now, and there were no more tears to wet it.

"The police think it's the mugger, honey," Bell said gently.

"Yes," Molly said. "I know what they think."

"Honey, I know you feel—"

"But what was she doing in Isola? Who took her to that deserted spot near the Hamilton Bridge? Did she go there alone, Peter?"

"I suppose so," Bell said.

"Why would she go there alone? Why would a seventeen-year-old girl go to a lonely spot like that?"

"I don't know, honey," Bell said. "Honey, please, don't get yourself all upset again. The police will find him. The police will—"

"Find *who?*" Molly said. "The mugger? But will they find whoever took her to that spot? Peter, it's all the way down in Isola. Why would she go there from Riverhead?"

Bell shook his head again. "I don't know, honey. I just don't know."

"We'll find him, Molly," Kling said. "Both Homicide North and the detectives in my precinct will be working on this one. Don't worry."

"And when you find him," Molly asked, "will that bring my sister back to life?"

Kling watched her, an old woman at twenty-four, sitting in her chair with her shoulders slumped, mourning a life, and carrying a life within her. They were silent for a long time. Finally Kling said he had to be leaving, and Molly graciously asked if he wouldn't like a cup of coffee. He said No, and he thanked her, and then he shook hands with Bell and went outside where the brittle afternoon sunlight washed the streets of Riverhead.

The kids were piling out of the junior high school up the street, and Kling watched them as he walked, young kids with clean-scrubbed faces, rowdy boys and pretty girls, chasing each other, shouting at each other, discovering each other.

Jeannie Paige had been a kid like this not many years ago.

He walked slowly.

There was a bite in the air, a bite that made him wish winter would come soon. It was a peculiar wish, because he truly loved autumn. It was strange, he supposed, because autumn was a time of dying, summer going quietly to rest, dying leaves, and dying days, and. . . .

Dying girls.

He shook the thought aside. On the corner opposite the junior high, a hot-dog cart stood, and the proprietor wore a white apron, and he owned a mustache and a bright smile, and he dipped his fork into the steaming frankfurter pot, and then into the sauerkraut pot, and then he put the fork down and took the round stick from the mustard jar and spread the mustard and handed the completed masterpiece to a girl of no more than fourteen who stood near the cart. She paid for the frankfurter, and there was pure joy on her face as she bit into it, and Kling watched her and then walked on.

A dog darted into the gutter, leaping and frisking, chasing a rubber ball that had bounced from the sidewalk. A car skidded to a stop, tires screeching, and the driver shook his head and then smiled unconsciously when he saw the happy pup.

The leaves fell toward the pavement, oranges and reds and yellows and russets and browns and pale golds, and they covered the sidewalks with crunching mounds.

He listened to the rasp of the leaves underfoot as he walked, and he sucked in the brisk fall air, and he thought, *It isn't fair; she had so much living to do.*

A cold wind came up when he hit the Avenue. He started for the elevated station, and the wind rushed through the jacket he wore, touching the marrow of his bones.

The voices of the junior-high-school kids were far behind him now, up De Witt Street, drowned in the controlled shriek of the new wind.

He wondered if it would rain.

The wind howled around him, and it spoke of secret tangled places, and it spoke of death, and he was suddenly colder than he'd been before, and he wished for the comforting warmth of a coat collar, because a chill suddenly worked its way up his spine to settle at the back of his neck like a cold, dead fish.

He walked to the station and climbed the steps and, curiously, he was thinking of Jeannie Paige.

7

The girl's legs were crossed.

She sat opposite Willis and Byrnes in the lieutenant's office on the second floor of the 87th Precinct. They were good legs. The skirt reached to just a shade below her knees, and Willis could not help noticing they were good legs. Sleek and clean, full-calved, tapering to slender ankles, enhanced by the high-heeled black-patent pumps.

The girl was a redhead, and that was good. Red hair is obvious hair. The girl had a pretty face, with a small Irish nose and green eyes. She listened to the men in serious silence, and you could feel intelligence on her face and in her eyes. Occasionally she sucked in a deep breath, and when she did, the severe cut of her suit did nothing to hide the sloping curve of her breast.

The girl earned $5,555 a year. The girl had a .38 in her purse.

The girl was a detective 2nd/grade, and her name was Eileen Burke, as Irish as her nose.

57

"You don't have to take this one if you don't want it, Miss Burke," Byrnes said.

"It sounds interesting," Eileen answered.

"Hal— Willis'll be following close behind all the way, you understand. But that's no guarantee he can get to you in time should anything happen."

"I understand that, sir," Eileen said.

"And Clifford isn't such a gentleman," Willis said. "He's beaten, and he's killed. Or at least we think so. It might not be such a picnic."

"We don't think he's armed, but he used something on his last job, and it wasn't his fist. So you see, Miss Burke . . ."

"What we're trying to tell you," Willis said, "is that you needn't feel any compulsion to accept this assignment. We would understand completely were you to refuse it."

"Are you trying to talk me *into* this or *out* of it?" Eileen asked.

"We're simply asking you to make your own decision. We're sending you out as a sitting duck, and we feel—"

"I won't be such a sitting duck with a gun in my bag."

"Still, we felt we should present the facts to you before—"

"My father was a patrolman," Eileen said. "Pops Burke, they called him. He had a beat in Hades Hole. In 1938, an escaped convict named Flip Danielsen took an apartment on Prime and North Thirtieth. When the police closed in, my father was with them. Danielsen had a Thompson sub-machine gun in the apartment with him, and the first round he fired caught my father in the stomach. My father died that night, and he died painfully, because stomach wounds are not easy ones." Eileen paused. "I think I'll take the job."

Byrnes smiled. "I knew you would," he said.

"Will we be the only pair? Eileen asked Willis.

"To start, yes. We're not sure how this'll work. I can't follow too close or Clifford'll panic. And I can't lag too far behind or I'll be worthless."

"Do you think he'll bite?"

"We don't know. He's been hitting in the precinct and getting away with it, so chances are he won't change his m.o.—unless this killing has scared him. And from what

58

the victims have given us, he seems to hit without any plan. He just waits for a victim and then pounces."

"I see."

"So we figured an attractive girl walking the streets late at night, apparently alone, might smoke him out."

"I see." Eileen let the compliment pass. There were about four million attractive girls in the city, and she knew she was no prettier than most. "Has there been any sex motive?" she asked.

Willis glanced at Byrnes. "Not that we can figure. He hasn't molested any of his victims."

"I was only trying to figure what I should wear," Eileen said.

"Well, no hat," Willis said. "That's for sure. We want him to spot that red hair a mile away."

"All right," Eileen said.

"Something bright, so I won't lose you—but nothing too flashy," Willis said. "We don't want the Vice Squad picking you up."

Eileen smiled. "Sweater and skirt?" she asked.

"Whatever you'll be most comfortable in."

"I've got a white sweater," she said. "That should be clearly visible to both you and Clifford."

"Yes," Willis said.

"Heels or flats?"

"Entirely up to you. You may have to—Well, he may give you a rough time. If heels will hamper you, wear flats."

"He can hear heels better," Eileen said.

"It's up to you."

"I'll wear heels."

"All right."

"Will anyone else be in on this? I mean, will you have a walkie-talkie or anything?"

"No," Willis said, "it'd be too obvious. There'll be just the two of us."

"And Clifford, we hope."

"Yes," Willis said.

Eileen Burke sighed. "When do we start?"

"Tonight?" Willis asked.

"I was going to have my hair done," Eileen said, smiling, "but I suppose that can wait." The smile broadened. "It isn't every girl who can be sure at least *one* man is following her."

"Can you meet me here?"

"What time?" Eileen asked.

"When the shift changes. Eleven-forty-five?"

"I'll be here," she said. She uncrossed her legs and rose. "Lieutenant," she said, and Byrnes took her hand.

"Be careful, won't you?" Byrnes said.

"Yes, sir. Thank you." She turned to Willis. "I'll see you later."

"I'll be waiting for you."

"Good-by now," she said, and she left the office. When she was gone, Willis asked, "What do you think?"

"I think she'll be okay," Byrnes said. "She's got a record of fourteen subway-masher arrests."

"Mashers aren't muggers," Willis said.

Byrnes nodded reflectively. "I think she'll be okay."

Willis smiled. "I think so, too," he said.

In the Squad Room outside, Detective Meyer was talking about cats.

"The tally is now up to twenty-four," he told Temple. "The damnedest thing the 33rd has ever come across."

Temple scratched his crotch. "And they got no lead yet, huh?"

"Not a single clue," Meyer said. He watched Temple patiently. Meyer was a very patient man.

"He just goes around grabbing cats," Temple said, shaking his head. "What would a guy want to steal cats for?"

"That's the big question," Meyer said. "What's the motive? He's got the 33rd going crazy. I'll tell you something, George, I'm glad this one isn't in our laps."

"Argh," Temple said, "I've had some goofy ones in my time, too."

"Sure, but *cats?* Have you ever had cats?"

"I had cats up telephone poles when I was walking a beat," Temple said.

"Everybody had cats up telephone poles," Meyer said. "But this is a man who's going around stealing cats from apartments. Now tell me, George, have you ever heard anything like that?"

"Never," Temple said.

"I'll let you know how it works out," Meyer promised. "I'm really interested in this one. Tell you the truth, I don't think they'll ever crack it."

"The 33rd is pretty good, ain't it?" Temple asked.

"There's a guy waiting outside," Havilland shouted from his desk. "Ain't nobody gonna see what he wants?"

"The walk'll do you good, Rog," Meyer said.

"I just took a walk to the water cooler," Havilland said, grinning. "I'm bushed."

"He's very anemic," Meyer said, rising. "Poor fellow, my heart bleeds for him." He walked to the slatted rail divider. A patrolman was standing there, looking into the Squad Room. "Busy, huh?" he asked.

"Soso," Meyer said indifferently, "What've you got?"

"An autopsy report for . . ." He glanced at the envelope. "Lieutenant Peter Byrnes."

"I'll take it," Meyer said.

"Sign this, will you?" the patrolman said.

"He can't write," Havilland answered, propping his feet up on the desk. Meyer signed for the autopsy report. The patrolman left.

An autopsy report is a coldly scientific thing.

It reduces flesh and blood to medical terms, measuring in centimeters, analyzing with calm aloofness. There is very little warmth and emotion in any autopsy report. There is no room for sentiment, no room for philosophizing. There is only one or more eight-and-one-half-by-eleven sheets of official-looking paper, and there are typewritten words on the sheets, and those words explain in straightforward medical English the conditions under which such and such a person met death.

The person whose death was open to medical scrutiny in the autopsy report which Meyer brought to the lieutenant was a young girl named Jeanne Rita Paige.

The words were very cold.

Death is not famous for its compassion.

The words read:

CORONER'S AUTOPSY REPORT

PAIGE, JEANNE RITA

Female, white, Caucasian. Apparent age, 21. Chronological age, 17. Apparent height, 64 inches. Apparent weight, 120 lbs.

GROSS INSPECTION:

Head and face:

a) FACE—Multiple contusions visible. Frontal area of skull reveals marked depression of the tablet of bone which measures approximately 10 cm; commencing 3 cm above the right orbit the depression then descends obliquely downward across the bridge of the nose and terminates in the mid-portion of the left maxilla.

There are marked hemorrhagic areas visible in the conjunctival areas of both eyes. Gross examination also reveals the presence of clotted blood within the nasal and otic orifices.

b) HEAD—There is an area of cerebral concussion with depression of tablet of bone which involves the left temporal region of the skull. The depression measures approximately 11 cm and runs obliquely downward from the bregma to a point 2 cm above and lateral to the superior aspect of left ear. There are multiple blood clots matted in the head hair.

Body:

The dorsal and ventral aspects of thorax and chest reveal multiple superficial abrasions and slight lacerations.

The right buttock reveals an area of severe abrasion.

The right lower extremity reveals a compound fracture of the distal portion of tibia and fibula with bone protruding through medial distal third of the extremity.

Examination of PELVIS grossly and internally reveals following:

1) No evidence of blood in vaginal vault.

2) No evidence of attempted forced entrance or coitus.

3) No evidence of seminal fluid or sperm de-

monstrable on gross and microscopic examination of vaginal secretions.

4) Uterus is spherical in outline grossly and measures approximately 13.5 × 10 × 7.5 cm.

5) Placental tissue as well as chorionic and decidual tissue are present.

6) A fetus measuring 7 cm long and weighing 29 gms is present.

IMPRESSIONS:

1) Death instantaneous due to blows inflicted upon skull and face. Cerebral concussion.

2) Multiple abrasions and lacerations inflicted over body and compound fracture of lower right extremity, tibia and fibula probably incurred by descent over cliff.

3) There is no evidence of sexual assault.

4) Examination of uterine contents reveals a three-month pregnant uterus.

8

He could not shake the dead girl from his mind. Back on the beat Monday morning, Kling should have felt soaring joy. He had been inactive for too long, and now he was back on the job, and the concrete and asphalt should have sung beneath his feet. There was life everywhere around him; teeming, crawling life. The precinct was alive with humanity, and in the midst of all this life, Kling walked his beat and thought of death.

The precinct started with the River Highway.

There a fringe of greenery turned red and burnt umber hugged the river, broken by an occasional tribute to World War I heroes and an occasional concrete bench. You could see the big steamers on the river, cruising slowly toward the docks farther downtown, their white smoke puffing up into the crisp fall air. An aircraft carrier lay anchored in the center of the river, long and flat, in relief against the stark brown cliffs on the other side. the excursion boats plied their idle autumn trade. Summer was dying, and with it the shouts and joyous revelry of the sun-seekers.

And up the river, like a suspended, glistening web of silver, the Hamilton Bridge regally arched over the swirling brown waters below, touching two states with majestic fingers.

At the base of the bridge, at the foot of a small stone-and-earth cliff, a seventeen-year-old girl had died. The ground had sucked up her blood, but it was still stained a curious maroon-brown.

The big apartment buildings lining the River Highway turned blank faces to the bloodstained earth. The sun was reflected from the thousands of windows in the tall buildings, buildings which still employed doormen and elevator operators, and the windows blinked across the river with fiery-eyed blindness. The governesses wheeled their baby carriages up past the synagogue on the corner, marching their charges south toward the Stem which pierced the heart of the precinct like a multicolored, multifeathered, slender, sharp arrow. There were groceries and five-and-tens, and movie houses, and delicatessens, and butchers, and jewelers, and candy stores on the Stem. There was also a cafeteria on one of the corners, and on any day of the week, Monday to Sunday, you could spot at least twenty-five junkies in that cafeteria, waiting for the man with the White God. The Stem was slashed up its middle by a wide, iron-pipe-enclosed island, broken only by the side streets which crossed it. There were benches on each street end of the island, and men sat on those benches and smoked their pipes, and women sat with shopping bags clutched to their abundant breasts, and sometimes the governesses sat with their carriages, reading paper-backed novels.

The governesses never wandered south of the Stem.

South of the Stem was Culver Avenue.

The houses on Culver had never been really fancy. Like poor and distant relatives of the buildings lining the river, they had basked in the light of reflected glory many years ago. But the soot and the grime of the city had covered their bumpkin faces, had turned them into city people, and they stood now with hunched shoulders and dowdy clothes, wearing mournful faces. There were a lot of churches on Culver Avenue. There were also a lot of bars. Both were frequented regularly by the Irish people who still clung to their neighborhood tenaciously—in spite of the Puerto Rican influx, in spite of the Housing Authority, which was condemning and knocking down dwellings with remarkable rapidity, leaving behind rubble-strewn open fields in which grew the city's only crop: rubbish.

The Puerto Ricans hunched in the side streets between Culver Avenue and Grover's Park. Here were the *bodegas, carnicerías, zapaterías, joyerías, cuchifritos* joints. Here was *La Vía de Putas*, "The Street of the Whores," as old as time, as thriving and prosperous as General Motors.

Here, bludgeoned by poverty, exploited by pushers and thieves and policemen alike, forced into cramped and dirty dwellings, rescued occasionally by the busiest fire department in the entire city, treated like guinea pigs by the social workers, like aliens by the rest of the city, like potential criminals by the police, here were the Puerto Ricans.

Light-skinned and dark-skinned. Beautiful young girls with black hair and brown eyes and flashing white smiles. Slender men with the grace of dancers. A people alive with warmth and music and color and beauty, six per cent of the city's population, crushed together in ghettos scattered across the face of the town. The ghetto in the 87th Precinct, sprinkled lightly with some Italians and some Jews, more heavily with the Irish, but predominantly Puerto Rican, ran south from the River Highway to the park, and then east and west for a total of thirty-five blocks. One-seventh of the total Puerto Rican population lived in the confines of the 87th Precinct. There were ninety thousand people in the streets Bert Kling walked.

The streets were alive with humanity.

And all he could think of was death.

He did not want to see Molly Bell, and when she came to him he was distressed.

She seemed frightened of the neighborhood, perhaps because there was life within her, and perhaps because she felt the instinctive, savagely protective urge of the mother-to-be. He had just crossed Tommy, a Puerto Rican kid whose mother worked in one of the candy

65

stores. The boy had thanked him, and Kling had turned to go back on the other side of the street again, and that was when he saw Molly Bell.

There was a sharp bite to the air on that September 18, and Molly wore a topcoat which had seen better days, even though those better days had begun in a bargain basement downtown. Because of her coming child, she could not button the severly tailored coat much further than her breasts, and she presented a curiously disheveled appearance; the limp blond hair, the tired eyes, the frayed coat buttoned from her throat over her full breasts, and then parting in a wide V from her waist to expose her bulging belly.

"Bert!" she called, and she raised her hand in a completely feminie gesture, recapturing for a fleeting instant the beauty that must have been hers several years back, looking in that instant the way her sister, Jeannie, had looked when she was alive.

He lifted his billet in a gesture of greeting, motioned for her to wait on the other side of the street, and then crossed to meet her. "Hello, Molly," he said.

"I went to the station house first," she said hurriedly. "They told me you were on the beat."

"Yes," he answered.

"I wanted to see you, Bert."

"All right," he said. They cut down one of the side streets, and then walked with the park on their right, the trees a blazing pyre against the gray sky.

"'allo, Bert," a boy shouted, and Kling waved his billet.

"Have you heard?" Molly asked. "About the autopsy report?"

"Yes," he said.

"I can't believe it," she told him.

"Well, Molly, they don't make mistakes."

"I know, I know." She was breathing heavily. He stared at her for a long moment.

"Listen, are you sure you should be walking around like this?"

"Yes, it's very good for me. The doctor said I should walk a lot."

"Well, if you get tired—"

"I'll tell you. Bert, will you help?"

66

He looked at her face. There was no panic in her eyes, and the grief, too, had vanished. There was only a steadfastness of purpose shining there, a calm resolve.

"What could I possibly do?" he asked.

"You're a cop," she said.

"Molly, the best cops in the city are working on this. Homicide North doesn't let people get away with murder. I understand one of the detectives from our precinct has been working with a policewoman for the past two days. They've—"

"None of these people knew my sister, Bert."

"I know, but—"

"You knew her, Bert."

"I only talked to her for a little while. I hardly—"

"Bert, these men who deal with death . . . My sister is only another corpse to them."

"That's not true, Molly. They see a lot of it, but that doesn't stop them from doing their best on each case. Molly, I'm just a patrolman. I *can't* fool around with this, even if I wanted to."

"Why not?"

"I'd be stepping on toes. I've got my beat. This is my beat, this is my job. My job isn't investigating a murder case. I can get into a lot of trouble for that, Molly."

"My sister got into a lot of trouble, too," Molly said.

"Ah, Molly," Kling sighed, "don't ask me, please."

"I'm asking you."

"I can't do anything. I'm sorry."

"Why did you come to see her?" Molly asked.

"Because Peter asked me to. As a favor. For old time's sake."

"I'm asking you for a favor too, Bert. Not for old time's sake. Only because my sister was killed, and my sister was just a young kid, and she deserved to live a little longer, Bert, just a little longer."

They walked in silence for a time.

"Bert?" Molly said.

"Yes."

"Will you please help?"

"I—"

"Your Homicide detectives think it was the mugger. Maybe it was, I don't know. But my sister was pregnant, and the mugger didn't do that. And my sister was killed at the foot of the Hamilton Bridge, and I want to know why she was there. The killer's cliff is a long way from where we live, Bert. Why was she there? Why? Why?"

"I don't know."

"My sister had friends, I know she had. Maybe her friends know. Doesn't a young girl have to confide in someone? A young girl with a baby inside her, a secret inside her? Doesn't she tell someone?"

"Are you interested in finding the killer," Kling asked, "—or the father of the child?"

Molly considered this gravely. "They may be one and the same," she said at last.

"I—I don't think that's likely, Molly."

"But it's a possibility, isn't it? And your Homicide detectives are doing nothing about that possibility. I've met them, Bert. They've asked me questions, and their eyes are cold, and their mouths are stiff. My sister is only a body with a tag on its toe. My sister isn't flesh and blood to them. She isn't now, and she never was."

"Molly—"

"I'm not blaming them. Their jobs . . . I know that death becomes a commodity to them, the way meat is a commodity to a butcher. But this girl is my sister!"

"Do you—do you know who her friends were?"

"I only know that she went to one club a lot. A cellar club, one of these teen-age—" Molly stopped. Her eyes met Kling's hopefully. "Will you help?"

"I'll try," Kling said, sighing. "Strictly on my own. After hours. I can't do anything officially, you understand that."

"Yes, I understand."

"What's the name of this club?"

"Club Tempo."

"Where is it?"

"Just off Peterson, a block from the Avenue. I don't know the address. All the clubs are clustered there in the side street, in the private houses." She paused. "I belonged to one when I was a kid, too."

"I used to go to their Friday-night socials," Kling said. "But I don't remember one called Tempo. It must be new."

"I don't know," Molly said. She paused. "Will you go?"

"Yes."

"When?"

"I don't knock off until four. I'll ride up to Riverhead then and see if I can find the place."

"Will you call me afterwards?"

"Yes, certainly."

"Thank you, Bert."

"I'm only a uniformed cop," Kling said. "I don't know if you've got anything to thank me for."

"I've got a lot to thank you for," she said. She squeezed his hand. "I'll be waiting for your call."

"All right," he said. He looked down at her. The walk seemed to have tired her. "Shall I call a cab for you?"

"No," she said, "I'll take the subway. Good-by, Bert. And thank you."

She turned and started up the street. He watched her. From the back, except for the characteristically tilted walk of the pregnant woman, you could not tell she was carrying. Her figure looked quite slim, from the back, and her legs were good.

He watched her until she was out of sight, and then he crossed the street and turned up one of the side streets, waving to some people he knew.

9

Unlike detectives, who figure out their own work schedules, patrolmen work within the carefully calculated confines of the eight-hour-tour system. They start with five consecutive tours from 8:00 A.M. to 4:00 P.M., and then they relax for fifty-six hours. When they return to work, they do another five tours from midnight to 8:00 A.M. after which another fifty-six-hour swing commences. The next five tours are from 4:00 P.M. to midnight. Comes the fifty-six-hour break once more, and then the cycle starts from the top again.

The tour system doesn't respect Saturdays, Sundays, or holidays. If a cop's tour works out that way, he may get Christmas off. If not, he walks his beat. Or he arranges a switch with a Jewish cop who wants Rosh Hashana off. It's something like working in an aircraft factory during wartime. The only difference is that cops find it a little more difficult to get life insurance.

Bert Kling started work that Monday morning at 7:45 A.M., the beginning of the tour cycle. He was relieved on post at 3:40 P.M. He went back to the house, changed to street clothes in the locker room down the hall from the Detective Squad Room, and then went out into the late-afternoon sunshine.

Ordinarily, Kling would have walked the beat a little more in his street clothes. Kling carried a little black loose-leaf pad in his back pocket, and into that pad he jotted down information from WANTED circulars and from the bulls in the precinct. He knew, for example, that there was a shooting gallery at 3112 North Eleventh. He knew that a suspected pusher was driving a powder-blue 1953 Cadillac with the license plate RX 42–10. He knew that a chain department store in the midtown area had been held up the night before, and he knew who was suspected of the crime. And he knew that a few good collars would put him closer to Detective 3rd/Grade, which, of course, he wanted to become.

So he ordinarily walked the precinct territory when he was off duty, a few hours each day, watching, snooping, unhampered by the shrieking blue of his uniform, constantly amazed by the number of people who didn't recognize him in street clothes.

Today he had something else to do, and so he ignored his extracurricular activities. Instead, he boarded a train and headed uptown to Riverhead.

He didn't have much trouble finding Club Tempo. He simply stopped into one of the clubs he'd known as a kid, asked where Tempo was, and was given directions.

Tempo covered the entire basement level of a three-story brick house off Peterson Avenue on Klausner Street. You walked up a concrete driveway toward a two-car garage at the back of the house, made an abrupt left turn, and found yourself face to face with the back of the house, the entrance doorway to the club, and a painted sign pierced with an elongated quarter note on a long black shaft.

The sign read:

Kling tried the knob. The door was locked. From somewhere inside the club, he heard the lyric, sonnet-like words to "Sh-Boom" blasting from a record player. He raised his fist and knocked. He kept knocking, realizing abruptly that all the *sh-booming* was drowning out his fist. He waited until the record had exhausted its serene, madrigal-like melody, and then knocked again.

"Yeah?" a voice called. It was a young voice, male.

"Open up," Kling said.

"Who is it?"

He heard footsteps approaching the door, and then a voice close by on the other side of the door. "Who is it?"

He didn't want to identify himself as a cop. If he were going to start asking questions, he didn't want a bunch of kids automatically on the defensive.

"Bert Kling," he said.

"Yeah?" the voice answered. "Who's Bert Kling?"

"I want to hire the club," Kling answered.

"Yeah?"

"Yeah."

"What for?"

"If you'll open the door, we can talk about it."

"Hey, Tommy," the voice yelled, "some guy wants to hire the club."

Kling heard a mumbled answer, and then the door lock clicked, and the door opened wide on a thin, blond boy of eighteen.

"Come on in," the boy said. He was holding a stack of records in his right hand, clutched tight against his chest. He wore a green sweater and dungaree pants. A white dress shirt, collar unbuttoned, showed above the V neck of the sweater. "My name's Hud. That's short for Hudson. Hudson Patt. Double *t*. Come on in."

Kling stepped down into the basement room. Hud watched him.

"You're kind of old, ain't you?" Hud asked at last.

"I'm practically decrepit," Kling replied. He looked

71

around. Whoever had decorated the room had done a good job with it. The pipes in the ceiling had been covered with plasterboard which had been painted white. The walls were knotty pine to a man's waist, plasterboard above that. Phonograph records, shellacked and then tacked to the white walls and ceiling, gave the impression of curious two-dimensional ballons that had drifted free of their vendor's strings. There were easy chairs and a long sofa scattered about the room. A record player painted white and then covered with black notes and a G clef and a musical staff stood alongside a wide arch through which a second room was visible. There was no one but Hud and Kling in either of the two rooms. Whoever Tommy was, he seemed to have vanished into thin air.

"Like it?" Hud asked, smiling.

"It's pretty," Kling said.

"We done it all ourselves. Bought all those records on the ceiling and walls for two cents each. They're real bombs—stuff the guy wanted to get rid of. We tried playing one of them. All we got was scratches. Sounded like London during an air raid."

"Which you no doubt remember clearly," Kling said.

"Huh?" Hud asked.

"Do you belong to this club?" Kling asked back.

"Sure. Only members are allowed down during the day. In fact, nonmembers ain't allowed down except on Friday and Sunday nights. We have socials then." He stared at Kling. His eyes were wide and blue. "Dancing, you know?"

"Yes, I know," Kling said.

"A little beer sometimes, too. Healthy. This is healthy recreation." Hud grinned. "Healthy recreation is what strong, red-blooded American teen-agers need, am I right?"

"Absolutely."

"That's what Dr. Mortesson says."

"Who?"

"Dr. Mortesson. Writes a column in one of the papers. Every day. Healthy recreation." Hud continued grinning. "So what do you want to hire the club for?" he asked.

"I belong to a group of war veterans," Kling said.

72

"Yeah?"

"Yeah. We're . . . uh . . . having a sort of a get-together, meet the wives, girl-friends, like that, you know."

"Oh, sure," Hud said.

"So we need a place."

"Why don't you try the American Legion hall?"

"Too big."

"Oh."

"I figured one of these cellar clubs. This is an unusually nice one."

"Yeah," Hud said. "Done it all ourselves." He walked over to the record player, seemed ready to put the records down, then turned, changing his mind. "Listen, for what night is this?"

"A Saturday," Kling said.

"That's good—because we have our socials on Friday and Sunday."

"Yes, I know," Kling said.

"How much you want to pay?"

"That depends. You're sure the landlord here won't mind our bringing girls down? Not that anything funny would be going on or anything, you understand. Half the fellows are married."

"Oh, certainly," Hud said, suddenly drawn into the fraternity of the adult. "I understand completely. I never once thought otherwise."

"But there *will* be girls."

"That's perfectly all right."

"You're sure?"

"Sure. We have girls here all the time. Our club is co-ed."

"Is that right?"

"That's a fact," Hud said. We got twelve girls belong to the club."

"Girls from the neighborhood?" Kling asked.

"Mostly. From around, you know. Here and there. None of them come from too far."

"Anybody I might know?" Kling asked.

Hud estimated Kling's age in one hasty glance. "I doubt it, mister," he said, the glowing bond of fraternal adulthood shattered.

"I used to live in this neighborhood," Kling lied.

73

"Took out a lot of girls around here. Wouldn't be surprised if some of the girls in your club aren't their younger sisters."

"Well, that's a possibility," Hud conceded.

"What are some of their names?"

"Why do you want to know, pal?" a voice from the archway said. Kling whirled abruptly. A tall boy walked through the arch and into the room, zipping up the fly on his jeans. He was excellently built, with wide shoulders bulging the seams of his T shirt, tapering down to a slender waist. His hair was chestnut brown, and his eyes were a deeper chocolate brown. He was extremely handsome, and he walked with arrogant knowledge of his good looks.

"Tommy?" Kling said.

"That's my name," Tommy said. "I didn't get yours."

"Bert Kling."

"Glad to know you," Tommy said. He watched Kling carefully.

"Tommy's president of Club Tempo," Hud put in. "He gave me the okay to hire the place to you. Provided the price was right."

"I was in the john," Tommy said. "Heard everything you said. Why're you so interested in our chicks?"

"I'm not interested," Kling answered. "Just curious."

"Your curiosity, pal, should concern itself only with hiring the club. Am I right, Hud?"

"Sure," Hud answered.

"What can you pay, pal?"

"How often did Jeannie Paige come down here, pal?" Kling said. He watched Tommy's face. The face did not change expression at all. A record slid from the stack Hud was holding, clattering to the floor.

"Who's Jeannie Paige?" Tommy said.

"A girl who was killed last Thursday night."

"Never heard of her," Tommy said.

"Think," Kling told him.

"I am thinking." Tommy paused. "You a cop?"

"What difference does it make?"

"This is a clean club," Tommy said. "We never had any trouble with the cops, and we don't want none. We ain't even had any trouble with the landlord, and he's a son of a bitch from wayback."

"Nobody's looking for trouble," Kling said. "I asked you how often Jeannie Paige came down here."

"Never," Tommy said. "Ain't that right, Hud?"

Hud, reaching for the pieces of the broken record, looked up. "Yeah, that's right, Tommy."

"Suppose I am a cop?" Kling said.

"Cops have badges."

Kling reached into his back pocket, opened his wallet, and showed the tin. Tommy glanced at the shield.

"Cop or no cop, this is still a clean club."

"Nobody said it was dirty. Stop bulging your weight-lifter muscles and answer my questions straight. When was Jeannie Paige down here last?"

Tommy hesitated for a long time. "Nobody here had anything to do with killing her," he said at last.

"Then she *did* come down?"

"Yes."

"How often?"

"Every now and then."

"How often?"

"Whenever there was socials. Sometimes during the week, too. We let her in 'cause one of the girls—" Tommy stopped.

"Go ahead, finish it."

"One of the girls knows her. Otherwise we wouldn't've let her in except on social nights. That's all I was gonna say."

"Yeah," Hud said, placing the broken record pieces on the player cabinet. "I think this girl was gonna put her up for membership."

"Was she here last Thursday night?" Kling asked.

"No," Tommy answered quickly.

"Try it again."

"No, she wasn't here. Thursday night is Work Night. Six kids from the club get the duty each week—different kids, you undersatnd. Three guys and three girls. The guys do the heavy work, and the girls do the curtains, the glasses, things like that. No outsiders are allowed on Work Night. In fact, no members except the kids who are working are allowed. That's how I know Jeannie Paige wasn't here."

"Were you here?"

"Yeah," Tommy said.

"Who else was here?"

"What difference does it make? Jeannie wasn't here."

"What about her girl-friend? The one she knows?"

"Yeah, she was here."

"What's her name?"

Tommy paused. When he answered, it had nothing whatever to do with Kling's question. "This Jeannie kid, like you got to understand her.. She never even *danced* with nobody down here. A real zombie. Pretty as sin, but an iceberg. Ten below, I'm not kidding."

"Why'd she come down then?"

"Ask me an easy one. Listen, even when she did come down, she never stayed long. She'd just sit on the side lines and watch. There wasn't a guy in this club wouldn'ta liked to dump her in the hay, but, Jesus, what a terrifying creep she was." Tommy paused. "Ain't that right, Hud?"

Hud nodded. "That's right. Dead and all, I got to say it. She was a regular icicle. A real spook. After a while, none of the guys even bothered askin' her to dance. We just let her sit."

"She was in another world," Tommy said. "I thought for a while she was a dope addict or something, I mean it. You know, you read about them in the papers all the time." He shrugged. "But it wasn't that. She was just a Martian, that's all." He shook his head disconsolately. "Such a piece, too."

"A terrifying creep," Hud said, shaking his head.

"What's her girl-friend's name?" Kling asked again.

A glance of muted understanding passed between Tommy and Hud. Kling didn't miss it, but he bided his time.

"You get a pretty girl like Jeannie was," Tommy said, "and you figure, Here's something. Pal, did you ever see her? I mean, they don't make them like that any—"

"What's her girl-friend's name?" Kling repeated, a little louder this time.

"She's an older girl," Tommy said, his voice very low.

"How old?"

"Twenty," Tommy said.

"That almost makes her middle-aged like me," Kling said.

"Yeah," Hud agreed seriously.

"What's her age got to do with it?"

"Well . . ." Tommy hesitated.

"For Christ's sake, what is it?" Kling exploded.

"She's been around," Tommy said.

"So?"

"So—so we don't want any trouble down here. This is a clean club. No, really, I'm not snowing you. So—so if once in a while we fool around with Claire—"

"Claire what?" Kling snapped.

"Claire—" Tommy stopped.

"Look," Kling said tightly, "let's just cut this crap, okay? A seventeen-year-old kid had her head smashed in, and I don't feel like playing around! Now what the hell is this girl's name, and say it damn fast!"

"Claire Townsend." Tommy wet his lips. "Look, if our mothers found out we were . . . well, you know . . . fooling around with Claire down here, well, Jesus. Look, can't we leave her out of this? What's to gain? Jesus, is there anything wrong with a little fun?"

"Nothing," Kling said. "Do you find murder funny? Do you find it comical, you terrifying creep?"

"No, but—"

"Where does she live?"

"Claire?"

"Yes."

"Right on Peterson. What's the address, Hud?"

"Seven twenty-eight, I think," Hud said.

"Yeah, that sounds about right. But look, Officer, leave us out of it, will you?"

"How many of you do I have to protect?" Kling said dryly.

"Well . . . only Hud and me, actually," Tommy said.

"The Bobbsey Twins."

"Huh?"

"Nothing." Kling started for the door. "Stay away from big girls," he said. "Go lift some weights."

"You'll leave us out of it?" Tommy called.

"I may be back," Kling said, and then he left them standing by the record player.

10

In Riverhead—and throughout the city for that matter—but especially in Riverhead, the cave-dwellers have thrown up a myriad number of dwellings which they call middle-class apartment houses. These buildings are usually constructed of yellow brick, and they are carefully set on the street so that no wash is seen hanging on the lines, except when an inconsiderate city transit authority constructs an elevated structure that cuts through back yards.

The fronts of the buildings are usually hung with a different kind of wash. Here is where the women gather. They sit on bridge chairs and stools and they knit and they sun themselves, and they talk, and their talk is the dirty wash of the apartment building. In three minutes flat, a reputation can be ruined by these Mesdames Defarge. The ax drops with remarkable abruptness, whetted by a friendly discussion of last night's mah-jong game. The head, with equally remarkable suddenness rolls into the basket, and the discussion idles on to topics like "Should birth control be practiced in the Virgin Isles?"

Autumn was a bold seductress on that late Monday afternoon, September 18. The women lingered in front of the buildings, knowing their hungry men would soon be home for dinner, but lingering nonetheless, savoring the tantalizing bite of the air. When the tall, blond man stopped in front of 728 Peterson, paused to check the address over the arched doorway, and then stepped into the foyer, speculation ran rife among the women knitters. After a brief period of consultation, one of the women—a girl named Birdie—was chosen to sidle unobtrusively into the foyer and, if the opportunity were ripe, perhaps casually follow the good-looking stranger upstairs.

Birdie, so carefully unobtrusive was she, missed her golden opportunity. By the time she had wormed her way into the inner foyer, Kling was nowhere in sight.

He had checked the name "Townsend" in the long row of brass-plated mailboxes, pushed the bell button, and then leaned on the inner door until an answering buzz released its lock mechanism. He had then climbed to the fourth floor, found Apartment 47, and pushed another button.

He was now waiting.

He pushed the button again.

The door opened suddenly. He had heard no approaching footsteps, and the sudden opening of the door surprised him. Unconsciously, he looked first to the girl's feet. She was barefoot.

"I was raised in the Ozarks," she said, following his glance. "We own a vacuum cleaner, a carpet sweeper, a broiler, a set of encyclopedias, and subscriptions to most of the magazines. Whatever you're selling, we've probably got it, and we're not interested in putting you through college."

Kling smiled. "I'm selling an automatic apple corer," he said.

"We don't eat apples," the girl replied.

"This one mulches the seeds, and converts them to fiber. The corer comes complete with an instruction booklet telling you how to weave fiber mats."

The girl raised a speculative eyebrow.

"It comes in six colors," Kling went on. "Toast Brown, Melba Peach, Tart Red—"

"Are you on the level?" the girl asked, puzzled now.

"Proofreader Blue," Kling continued, "Bilious Green, and Midnight Dawn." He paused. "Are you interested?"

"Hell, no," she said, somewhat shocked.

"My name is Bert Kling," he said seriously. "I'm a cop."

"Now you sound like the opening to a television show."

"May I come in?"

"Am I in trouble?" the girl asked. "Did I leave that damn shebang in front of a fire hydrant?"

"No."

And then, as an afterthought, "Where's your badge?" Kling showed her his shield.

"You're supposed to ask," the girl said. "Even the man from the gas company. Everybody's supposed to carry identification like that."

"Yes, I know."

"So come in," she said. "I'm Claire Townsend."

"I know."

"How do you know?"

"The boys at Club Tempo sent me here."

Claire stared at Kling levelly. She was a tall girl. Even barefoot, she reached to Kling's shoulder. In high heels, she would give the average American male trouble. Her hair was black. Not brunette, not brownette, but black, a total black, the black of a starless, moonless night. Her eyes were a deep brown, arched with black brows. Her nose was straight, and her cheeks were high, and there wasn't a trace of make-up on her face, not a tint of lipstick on her wide mouth. She wore a white blouse, and black toreador pants, which tapered down to her naked ankles and feet. Her toenails were painted a bright red.

She kept staring at him. At last, she said, "Why'd they send you here?"

"They said you knew Jeannie Paige."

"Oh." The girl seemed ready to blush. She shook her head slightly, as if to clear it of an erroneous first impression, and then said, "Come in."

Kling followed her into the apartment. It was furnished with good middle-class taste.

"Sit down," she said.

"Thank you." He sat in a low easy chair. It was difficult to sit erect, but he managed it. Claire went to the coffee table, shoved the lid off a cigarette box, took one of the cigarettes for herself, and then asked, "Smoke?"

"No, thanks."

"Your name was Kling, did you say?"

"Yes."

"You're a detective?"

"No. A patrolman."

"Oh." Claire lighted the cigarette, shook out the match, and then studied Kling. "What's your connection with Jeannie?"

"I was about to ask you the same thing."

Claire grinned. "I asked first."

"I know her sister. I'm doing a favor."

80

"Um-huh." Claire nodded, digesting this. She puffed on the cigarette, folded her arms across her breasts and then said, "Well, go ahead. Ask the questions. You're the cop."

"Why don't you sit down?"

"I've been sitting all day."

"You work?"

"I'm a college girl," Claire said. "I'm studying to be a social worker."

"Why that?"

"Why not?"

Kling smiled. "This time, *I* asked first."

"I want to get to people before you do," she said.

"That sounds reasonable," Kling said. "Why do you belong to Club Tempo?"

Her eyes grew suddenly wary. He could almost see a sudden film pass over the pupils, masking them. She turned her head and blew out a ball of smoke. "Why shouldn't I?" she asked.

"I can see where our conversation is going to run around in the why—why not rut," Kling said.

"Which is a damn sight better than the why—because rut, don't you think?" There was an edge to her voice now. He wondered what had suddenly changed her earlier friendliness. He weighed her reaction for a moment, and then decided to plunge onward.

"The boys there are a little young for you, aren't they?"

"You're getting a little personal, aren't you?"

"Yes," Kling said. "I am."

"Our acquaintance is a little short for personal exchanges," Claire said icily.

"Hud can't be more than eighteen—"

"Listen—"

"And what's Tommy? Nineteen? They haven't got an ounce of brains between them. Why do you belong to Tempo?"

Claire squashed out her cigarette. "Maybe you'd better leave, Mr. Kling," she said.

"I just got here," he answered.

She turned. "Let's set the record straight. So far as I know, I'm not obliged to answer any questions you ask about my personal affairs, unless I'm under suspicion for some foul crime. To bring the matter down to a fine technical point, I don't have to answer *any* questions a patrolman asks me, unless he is operating in an official capacity, which you admitted you were not. I liked Jeannie Paige, and I'm willing to cooperate. But if you're going to get snotty, this is still my home, and my home is my castle, and you can get the hell out."

"Okay," Kling said, embarrassed. "I'm sorry, Miss Townsend."

"Okay," Claire said. A silence clung to the atmosphere. Claire looked at Kling. Kling looked back at her.

"I'm sorry, too," Claire said finally. "I shouldn't be so goddamn touchy."

"No, you were perfectly right. It's none of my business what you—"

"Still, I shouldn't have—"

"No, really, it's—"

Claire burst out laughing, and Kling joined her. She sat, still chuckling, and said, "Would you like a drink, Mr. Kling?"

Kling looked at his watch. "No, thanks," he said.

"Too early for you?"

"Well—"

"It's never too early for cognac," she said.

"I've never tasted cognac," he admitted.

"You haven't?" Her eyebrows shot up onto her forehead. "Ah, monsieur, you are meesing one of ze great treats of life. A little, *oui? Non?*"

"A little," he said.

She crossed to a bar with green leatherette doors, opened them, and drew out a bottle with a warm, amber liquid showing within.

"Cognac," she announced grandly, "the king of brandies. You can drink it as a highball, cocktail, punch—or in coffee, tea, hot chocolate, and milk."

"Milk?" Kling asked, astonished.

"Milk, yes indeed. But the best way to enjoy cognac is to sip it—neat."

"You sound like an expert," Kling said.

Again, quite suddenly, the veil passed over her eyes. "Someone taught me to drink it," she said flatly, and then she poured some of the liquid into two medium-sized, tulip-shaped glasses. When she turned to face Kling again, the mask had dropped from her eyes.

"Note that the glass is only half filled," she said. "That's so you can twirl it without spilling any of the drink." She handed the glass to Kling. "The twirling motion mixes the cognac vapors with the air in the glass, bringing out the bouquet. Roll the glass in your palms, Mr. Kling. That warms the cognac and also brings out the aroma."

"Do you smell this stuff or drink it?" Kling wanted to know. He rolled the glass between his big hands.

"Both," Claire said. "That's what makes it a good experience. Taste it. Go ahead."

Kling took a deep swallow, and Claire opened her mouth and made an arupt "Stop!" signal with one outstretched hand. "Good God," she said, "don't gulp it! You're committing an obscenity when you gulp cognac. Sip it, roll it around your tongue."

"I'm sorry," Kling apologized. He sipped the cognac, rolled it on his tongue. "Good," he said.

"Virile," she said.

"Velvety," he added.

"End of commercial."

They sat silently, sipping the brandy. He felt very cozy and very warm and very comfortable. Claire Townsend was a pleasant person to look at, and a pleasant person to talk to. Outside the apartment, the shadowy grays of autumn dusk were washing the sky.

"About Jeannie," he said. He did not feel like discussing death.

"Yes?"

"How well did you know her?"

"As well as anyone, I suppose. I don't think she had many friends."

"What makes you say that?"

"You can tell. That lost-soul look. A beautiful kid, but lost. God, what I wouldn't have given for the looks she had."

"You're not so bad," Kling said, smiling. He sipped more brandy.

"That's the warm, amber glow of the cognac," Claire advised him. "I'm a beast in broad daylight."

"I'll just bet you are," Kling said. "How'd you first meet her?"

"At Tempo. She came down one night. I think her boyfriend sent her. In any case, she had the name of the club and the address written on a little white card. She showed it to me, almost as if it were a ticket of admission, and then she just sat in the corner and refused dances. She looked. . . . It's hard to explain. She was there, but she wasn't there. Have you seen people like that?"

"Yes," Kling said.

"I'm like that myself sometimes," Claire admitted. "Maybe that's why I spotted it. Anyway, I went over and introduced myself and we started talking. We got along very well. By the end of the evening we'd exchanged telephone numbers."

"Did she ever call you?"

"No. I only saw her at the club."

"How long ago was this?"

"Oh, a long time now."

"How long?"

"Let me see." Claire sipped her cognac and thought. "Gosh, it must be almost a year." She nodded. "Yes, just about."

"I see. Go ahead."

"Well, it wasn't hard to find out what was troubling her. The kid was in love."

Kling leaned forward. "How do you know?"

Claire's eyes did not leave his face. "I've been in love, too," she said tiredly.

"Who was her boy-friend?" Kling asked.

"I don't know."

"Didn't she tell you?"

"No."

"Didn't she mention his name ever? I mean, in conversation?"

"No."

"Hell," Kling said.

"Understand, Mr. Kling, that this was a new bird taking wing. Jeannie was leaving the nest, testing her feathers."

"I see."

"Her first love, Mr. Kling, and shining in her eyes,

84

and glowing on her face, and putting her in this dream world of hers where everthing outside it was shadowy." Claire shook her head. "God, I've seen them green, but Jeannie—" She stopped and shook her head again. "She just didn't know anything, do you know? Here was this woman's body. . . . Well, had you ever seen her?"

"Yes."

"Then you know what I mean. This was the real item, a woman. But inside—a little girl."

"How do you figure that?" Kling asked, thinking of the autopsy results.

"Everything about her. The way she used to dress, the way she talked, the questions she asked, even her handwriting. All a little girl's. Believe me, Mr. Kling, I've never—"

"Her handwriting?"

"Yes, yes. Here, let me see if I've still got it." She crossed the room and scooped her purse from a chair. "I'm the laziest girl in the world. I never copy an address into my address book. I just stick it in between the pages until I've. . . ." She was thumbing through a little black book. "Ah, here it is," she said. She handed Kling a white card. "She wrote that for me the night we met. Jeannie Paige, and then the phone number. Now, look at the way she wrote."

Kling looked at the card in puzzlement. "This says 'Club Tempo,'" he said. "'Eighteen twelve Klausner Street.'"

"What?" Claire frowned. "Oh, yes. That's the card she came down with that night. She used the other side to give me her number. Turn it over."

Kling did.

"See the childish scrawl? That was Jeannie Paige a year ago."

Kling flipped the card over again. "I'm more interested in *this* side," he said. "You told me you thought her boy-friend might have written this. Why do you say that?"

"I don't know. I just assumed he was the person who sent her down, that's all. It's a man's handwriting."

"Yes," Kling said. "May I keep this?"

Claire nodded. "If you like." She paused. "I guess I have no further use for Jeannie's phone number."

"No," Kling said. He put the card into his wallet. "You said she asked you questions. What kind of questions?"

"Well, for one, she asked me how to kiss."

"What?"

"Yes. She asked me what to do with her lips, whether she should open her mouth, use her tongue. And all this delivered with that wide-eyed, baby-blue stare. It sounds incredible, I know. But, remember, she was a young bird, and she didn't know how strong her wings were."

"She found out," Kling said.

"Huh?"

"Jeannie Paige was pregnant when she died."

"No!" Claire said. She put down the brandy glass. "No, you're joking!"

"I'm serious."

Claire was silent for several moments. Then she said, "First time at bat, and she gets beaned. Damnit! God-damnit!"

"But you don't know who her boy-friend was?"

"No."

"Had she continued seeing him? You said this was a year ago. I mean—"

"I know what you mean. Yes, the same one. She'd been seeing him regularly. In fact, she used the club for that."

"He came to the club!" Kling said, sitting erect.

"No, no." Claire was shaking her head impatiently. "I think her sister and brother-in-law objected to her seeing this fellow. So she told them she was going down to Tempo. She'd stay there a little while, just in case anyone was checking, and then she'd leave."

"Let me understand this," Kling said. "She came to the club, and then left to meet him. Is that right?"

"Yes."

"This was standard procedure? This happened each time she came down?"

"Almost each time. Once in a while she'd stay at the club until things broke up."

"Did she meet him in the neighborhood?"

"No, I don't think so. I walked her down to the El once."

"What time did she generally leave the club?"

"Between ten and ten-thirty."

"And she walked to the El, is that right? And you assume she took a train there and went to meet him."

"I *know* she went to meet him. The night I walked her, she told me she was going downtown to meet him."

"Downtown where?"

"She didn't say."

"What did he look like, this fellow?"

"She didn't say."

"She never described him?"

"Only to say he was the handsomest man in the world. Look, who ever describes his love? Shakespeare, maybe. That's all."

"Shakespeare and seventeen-year-olds," Kling said. "Seventeen-year-olds shout their love to the rooftops."

"Yes," Claire said gently. "Yes."

"But not Jeannie Paige. Damnit, why not her?"

"I don't know." Claire thought for a moment. "This mugger who killed her—"

"Um?"

"The police don't think he was the fellow she was seeing, do they?"

"This is the first anyone connected with the police is hearing about her love life," Kling said.

"Oh. Well, he—he didn't sound that way. He sounded gentle. I mean, when Jeannie did talk about him, he sounded gentle."

"But she never mentioned his name?"

"No. I'm sorry."

Kling rose. "I'd better be going. That *is* dinner I smell, isn't it?"

"My father'll be home soon," Claire said. "Mom is dead. I whip something up when I get home from school."

"Every night?" Kling asked.

"What? I'm sorry . . ."

He didn't know whether to press it or not. She hadn't heard him, and he could easily have shrugged his comment aside. But he chose not to.

"I said, 'Every night?' "

"Every night what?"

She certainly was not making it easy for him. "Do you prepare supper every night? Or do you occasionally get a night off?"

"Oh, I get nights off," Claire said.

"Maybe you'd enjoy dinner out some night?"

"With you, do you mean?"

"Well, yes. Yes, that's what I had in mind."

Claire Townsend looked at him long and hard. At last she said, "No, I don't think so. I'm sorry. Thanks. I couldn't."

"Well . . . uh . . ." Quite suddenly, King felt like a horse's ass. "I . . . uh . . . guess I'll be going then. Thanks for the cognac. It was very nice."

"Yes," she said, and he remembered her discussing people who were there and yet not there, and he knew exactly what she meant because she was not there at all. She was somewhere far away, and he wished he knew where. With sudden, desperate longing, he wished he knew where she was because, curiously, he wanted to be there with her.

"Good-by," he said.

She smiled in answer, and closed the door behind him.

The dime in the slot brought him Peter Bell.

Bell's voice was sleepy. "I didn't wake you, did I?" Kling asked.

"Yes, you did," Bell said, "but that's all right. What is it, Bert?"

"Well, is Molly there?"

"Molly? No. She went down to pick up a few things. What is it?"

"I've been—well, she asked me to check around a little."

"Oh? Did she?"

"Yeah. I went to Club Tempo this afternoon, and I also talked with a girl named Claire Townsend. Nice girl."

"What did you find out, Bert?"

"That Jeannie was seeing some guy regularly."

"Who?"

"Well, that's just it. Miss Townsend didn't know. She ever mention anybody's name to you or Molly?"

"No, not that I can remember."

"That's too bad. Might give me something to go on, you know. If we had even a first name. Something to work with."

"No," Bell said, "I'm sorry but—" He stopped dead. There was painful silence on the line, and then he said, "Oh, my God!"

"What's the matter?"

"She did, Bert. She *did* mention someone. Oh my God!"

"Who? When was this?"

"We were talking once. She was in a good mood, and she told me—Bert, she told me the name of the fellow she was seeing."

"What was the name?"

"Clifford! Holy Jesus, Bert! His name is Clifford!"

11

It was Roger Havilland who brought in the first real suspect in the alleged mugger murder.

The suspect was a kid named Sixto Fangez, a Puerto Rican boy who had been in the city for a little more than two years. Sixto was twenty years old, and had until recently been a member of a street gang known as "The Tornadoes." He was no longer active, having retired in favor of marriage to a girl named Angelita. Angelita was pregnant.

Sixto had allegedly beat up a hooker and stolen thirty-two dollars from her purse. The girl was one of the better-known prostitutes in the precinct territory and had, in fact, rolled in the hay on a good many occasions with members of the legion in blue. Some of these policemen had paid her for the privilege of her company.

In ordinary circumstances, in spite of the fact that the girl had made a positive indentification of Sixto Fangez, Havilland might have been willing to forget the whole matter in consideration of a little legal tender. Assault charges had been known to slip the minds of many policemen when the right word together with the right amount of currency was exchanged.

It happened, however, that the newspapers were giving a big play to the funeral of Jeannie Paige—a funeral which had been delayed by the extensive autopsy examination performed on the body—on the morning that Sixto was brought upstairs to the Squad Room. The newspapers were also pressuring the cops to do something about the rampant mugger, and so perhaps Havilland's extreme enthusiam could have been forgiven.

He booked a bewildered and frightened Sixto, barked "Follow me!" over his shoulder, and then led him to a room politely marked INTERROGATION. Inside the room, Havilland locked the door and calmly lighted a cigarette. Sixto watched him. Havilland was a big man who, in his own words, "took crap from nobody." He had once started to break up a street fight and had in turn had his arm broken in four places. The healing process, considering the fact that the bones would not set properly the first time and had to be rebroken and reset, was a painful thing to bear. The healing process had given Havilland a lot of time to think. He thought mostly about being a good cop. He thought also about survival. He formed a philosophy.

Sixto was totally unaware of the thinking process which had led to the formation of Havilland's credo. He only knew that Havilland was the most hated and the most feared cop in the barrio. He watched him with interest, a light film of sweat beading his thin upper lip. His eyes never left Havilland's hands.

"Looks like you're in a little trouble, huh, Sixto?" Havilland said.

Sixto nodded, his eyes blinking. He wet his lips.

"Now, why'd you go and beat up on Carmen, huh?" Havilland said. He leaned against the table in the room, leisurely blowing out a stream of smoke. Sixto, thin, birdlike, wiped his bony hands on the coarse tweed of his trousers. Carmen was the prostitute he'd allegedly mugged. He knew that she had on occasion been friendly with the bulls. He did not know the extent of her relationship with Havilland. He maintained a calculating silence.

"Huh?" Havilland asked pleasantly, his voice unusually soft. "Now why'd you go and beat up on a nice-looking little girl like Carmen?"

Sixto remained silent.

"Were you looking for some trim, huh, Sixto?"

"I am married," Sixto said formally.

"Looking for a little gash, huh, Sixto?"

"No, I am married. I don't go to the prostitutes," Sixto said.

"What were you doing with Carmen then?"

"She owe me money," Sixto said. "I wenn to collec' it."

"You lent her money, is that right, Sixto?"

"*Sí,*" Sixto said.

"How much money?"

"Abou' forty dollars."

"And so you went to her and tried to collect it, is that right?"

"*Sí.* Iss my money. I lenn it to her maybe three, maybe four munns ago."

"Why'd she need it, Sixto?"

"Hell, she's a junkie. Don't you know that?"

"I heard something along those lines," Havilland said, smiling pleasantly. "So she needed a fix and she came to you for the loot, that right, Sixto?"

"She dinn come to me. I happen to be sittin' in the bar, an' she say she wass low, so I lay the forty on her. Thass all. So now I wenn aroun' to collec' it. So she give me a hard time."

"What kind of a hard time?"

"She say business iss bad, an' she don't get many johns comin' from downtown, an' like that. So I tell her I don't care abou' her business. All I wann is my forty dollars back. I'm a married man. I'm gonna have a baby soon. I cann fool aroun' lennin money to hookers."

"You working, Sixto?"

"*Sí.* I work in a res'aurant downtown."

"How come you needed this forty bucks so bad right now?"

"I tol' you. My wife's pregin. I got doctor bills, man."

"So why'd you hit Carmen?"

"Because I tell her I don't have to stann aroun' bullin' with a hooker. I tell her I wann my money. So she come back and say my Angelita iss a hooker, too! Christ, man, thass my wife. Angelita! She's clean like the Virgin Mary! So I bust her in the mouth. Thass what happen."

"And then you went through her purse, huh, Sixto?"

"Only to get my forty dollars."

"And you got thirty-two, right?"

"*Sí*. She still owe me eight."

Havilland nodded sympathetically, and then slid an ashtray across the table top. With small, sharp stabs, he stubbed out his cigarette. He looked up at Sixto then, a smile on his cherubic face. He sucked in a deep breath, his massive shoulders heaving.

"Now what's the real story, Sixto?" he said softly.

"Thass the real story," Sixto said. "Thass the way it happen."

"What about these other girls you've been mugging?"

Sixto looked at Havilland unblinkingly. For a moment, he seemed incapable of speech. Then he said, "What?"

"These other girls all over the city? How about it, Sixto?"

"What?" Sixto said again.

Havilland moved off the table gracefully. He took three steps to where Sixto was standing. Still smiling, he brought his fist back and rammed the knuckles into Sixto's mouth.

The blow caught Sixto completely by surprise. His eyes opened wide, and he felt himself staggering backward. Then he collided with the wall and automatically wiped the back of his hand across his mouth. A red smear stained the tan of his fingers. He blinked his eyes and looked across at Havilland.

"What for you hit me?" he asked.

"Tell me about the other girls, Sixto," Havilland said, moving toward him again.

"*What* other girls? Jesus, what are you crazy or something? I hit a hooker to get back my—"

Havilland lashed out backhanded, then swung his open palm around to catch Sixto's other cheek. Again the hand lashed back, forward, back, forward, until Sixto's head was rocking like a tall blade of grass in a stiff breeze. He tried to cover his face, and Havilland jabbed out at his stomach. Sixto doubled over in pain.

"Ave Maria," he said, "why are you—"

"Shut up!" Havilland shouted. "Tell me about the muggings, you spic son of a bitch! Tell me about that seventeen-year-old blonde you killed last week!"

"I dinn kill—"

Havilland hit him again, throwing his huge fist at Sixto's head. He caught Sixto under the eye, and the boy fell to the floor, and Havilland kicked him with the point of his shoe.

"Get up."

"I dinn—"

Havilland kicked him again. The boy was sobbing now. He climbed to his feet, and Havilland punched him once in the stomach and then in the face. Sixto crumpled against the wall, sobbing wildly.

"Why'd you kill her?"

Sixto couldn't answer. He kept shaking his head over and over again, sobbing. Havilland seized his jacket front and began pounding the boy's head agaisnt the wall.

"Why you friggin spic? Why? Why? Why?"

But Sixto only kept shaking his head, and after a while his head lolled to one side, and he was unconscious.

Havilland studied him for a moment. He let out a deep sigh, went to the washbasin in the corner, and washed the blood from his hands. He lighted a cigarette then and went to the table, sitting on it and thinking. It was a damn shame, but he didn't think Sixto was the man they wanted. They still had him on the Carmen thing, of course, but they couldn't hang this mugger kill on him. It was a damn shame.

In a little while, Havilland unlocked the door and went next door to Clerical. Miscolo looked up from his typewriter.

"There's a spic next door," Havilland said, puffing on his cigarette.

"Yeah?" Miscolo said.

Havilland nodded. "Yeah. Fell down and hurt himself. Better get a doctor, huh?"

In another part of the city, a perhaps more orthodox method of questioning was being undertaken by Detectives Meyer and Temple.

Meyer, personally, was grateful for the opportunity. In accordance with Lieutenant Byrnes' order, he had been questioning known sex offenders until he was blue in the face. It was not that he particularly disliked questioning; it was simply that he disliked sex offenders.

The sunglasses found alongside the body of Jeannie Paige had borne a small "C" in a circle over the bridge. The police had contacted several jobbers, one of whom identified the © as the trade-mark of a company known as Candrel, Inc. Byrnes had extricated Meyer and Temple from the sticky, degenerate web at the 87th, and sent them shuffling off to Majesta, where the firm's factory was located.

The office of Geoffrey Candrel was on the third floor of the factory, a soundproofed rectangle of knotty-pine walls and modern furniture. The desk seemed suspended in space. A painting on the wall behind the desk resembled an electronic computing machine with a nervous breakdown.

Candrel was a fat man in a big leather chair. He looked at the broken sunglasses on his desk, shoved at them with a pudgy forefinger as if he were prodding a snake to see if it were sill alive.

"Yes," he said. His voice was thick. It rumbled up out of his huge chest. "Yes, we manufacture those glasses."

"Can you tell us something about them?" Meyer asked.

"Can I tell you something about them?" Candrel smiled in a peculiarly superior manner. "I've been making frames for *all* kinds of glasses for more than fourteen years now. And you ask me if I can tell you something about them? My friend, I can tell you whatever you want to know."

"Well, can you tell us—"

"The trouble with most people," Candrel went on, "is that they think it's a simple operation to make a pair of sunglass frames—or any kind of eyeglass frames for that matter. Well, gentlemen, that's simply not true. Unless you're a sloppy workman who doesn't give a damn about the product you're putting out. Candrel gives a damn. Candrel considers the consumer."

"Well, perhaps you can—"

"We get this sheet stock first," Candrel said, ignoring

94

Meyer. "It's called zyl—that's the trade term for cellulose nitrate, optical grade. We die-stamp the fronts and temple shapes from that sheet stock."

"Fronts?" Meyer said.

"Temples?" Temple said.

"The front is the part of the eyeglasses that holds the lenses. The temples are the two gizmos you put over your ears."

"I see," Meyer said. "But about these glasses—"

"After they're stamped, the fronts and temples are machined," Candrel said, "to put the groves in the rims, and to knock off the suqare edges left by the stamping. Then the nose pads are cemented to the fronts. After that, a cutter blends the pads to the fronts in a 'phrasing' operation."

"Yes, sir, but—"

"Nor is that the end of it," Candrel said. "To blend the nose pads further, they are rubbed on a wet pumice wheel. Then the fronts and temples go through a roughing operation. They're put into a tumbling barrel of pumice, and the tumbling operation takes off all the rough machine marks. In the finishing operation, these same fronts and temples are put into a barrel of small wooden pegs—about an inch long by three-sixteenths of an inch wide—together with a lubricant and our own secret compound. The pegs slide over the fronts and temples, polishing them."

"Sir, we'd like to get on with—"

"After that," Candrel said, frowning, a man obviously not used to being interrupted, "the fronts and temples are slotted for hinges, and then the hinges are fastened with shields, and then fronts are assembled to temples with screws. The corners are mitered, and then the ends are rounded on a pumice wheel in the Rubbing Room. After that—"

"Sir—"

"After that, the frames are washed and cleaned and sent to the Polishing Room. All of our frames are *hand-polished*, gentlemen. A lot of companies simply dip the frames into a solvent to give it a polished look. Not us. We *hand-polish* them."

"That's admirable, Mr. Candrel," Meyer said, "but—"

"And when we insert plain glass lenses, we use a six base

lens, a lens that has been ground and is without distortion. Our plano sunglasses are six-diopter lenses, gentlemen. And remember, *a six-base lens is optically correct.*"

"I'm sure it is," Meyer said tiredly.

"Why, our best glasses retail for as high as twenty dollars," Candrel said proudly.

"What about these?" Meyer asked, pointing to the glasses on Candrel's desk.

"Yes," Candrel said. He poked at the glasses with his finger again. "Of course, we also put out a cheaper line. We injection-mold them out of polystyrene. It's a high-speed die-casting operation done under hydraulic pressure. Semiautomatic, you understand. And, of course, we use less expensive lenses."

"Are these glasses a part of your cheaper line?" Meyer asked.

"Ah . . . yes." Candrel seemed suddenly embarrassed.

"How much do they cost?"

"We sell them to our jobbers for thirty-five cents a pair. They probably retail anywhere from seventy-five cents to a dollar."

"What about your distribution?" Temple asked.

"Sir?"

"Where are these glasses sold? Any particular stores?"

Candrel pushed the glasses clear to the other side of his desk, as if they had grown suddenly leprous.

"Gentlemen," he said, "you can buy these glasses in any five-and-ten-cent store in the city."

12

At two o'clock on the morning of Thursday, September 21, Eileen Burke walked the streets of Isola in a white sweater and a tight skirt.

She was a tired cop.

She had been walking the streets of Isola since eleven-forty-five the previous Saturday night. This was her fifth night of walking. She wore high-heeled pumps, and they had definitely not been designed for hikes. In an attempt to lure the mugger, whose basic motivation in choosing women might or might not have been sexually inspired, she had hitched up her brassière a notch or two higher so that her breasts were cramped and upturned, albeit alluring.

The allure of her mammary glands was not to be denied by anyone, least of all someone with so coldly analytical a mind as Eileen Burke possessed.

During the course of her early-morning promenades, she had been approached seven times by sailors, four times by soldiers, and twenty-two times by civilians in various styles of male attire. The approaches had ranged from polite remarks such as, "Nice night, ain't it?" to more direct opening gambits like, "Walking all alone, honey?" to downright unmistakable business inquires like. "How much, babe?"

All of these, Eileen had taken in stride.

They had, to be truthful, broken the monotony of her otherwise lonely and silent excursions. She had never once caught sight of Willis behind her, though she knew with certainty that he was there. She wondered now if he was as bored as she, and she concluded that he was possibly not. He did, after all, have the compensating sight of a backside which she jiggled jauntily for the benefit of any unseen, observant mugger.

Where are you, Clifford? she mentally asked.

Have we scared you off? Did the sight of the twisted and bloody young kid whose head you split open turn your stomach, Clifford? Have you decided to give up this business, or are you waiting until the heat's off?

Come on, Clifford.

See the pretty wiggle? The bait is yours, Clifford. And the only hook is the .38 in my purse.

Come on, Clifford!

From where Willis jogged doggedly along behind Eileen, he could make out only the white sweater and occasionally a sudden burst of bright red when the lights caught at her hair.

He was a tired cop.

It had been a long time since he'd walked a beat, and this was worse than walking any beat in the city. When you had a beat, you also had bars and restauraunts and sometimes tailor shops or candy stores. And in those places you could pick up, respectively, a quick beer, cup of coffee, snatch of idle conversation, or warmth from a hissing radiator.

This girl Eileen liked walking. He had followed behind her for four nights now, and this was the fifth, and she hadn't once stopped walking. This was an admirable attitude, to be sure, a devotion to duty which was not to be scoffed aside.

But good Christ, man, did she have a motor?

What propelled those legs of hers? (Good legs, Willis. Admit it.)

And why so fast? Did she think Clifford was a cross-country track star? He had spoken to her about her speed after their first night of breakneck pacing. She had smiled easily, fluffed her hair like a virgin at a Freshman tea and said, "I always walk fast."

That, he thought now, had been the understatement of the year.

What she meant, of course, was, "I always *run* slow."

He did not envy Clifford. Whoever he was, wherever he was, he would need a motorcycle to catch this redhead with the paperback-cover bazooms.

Well, he thought, she's making the game worth the candle.

Wherever you are, Clifford, Miss Burke's going to give you a run for your money.

He had first heard the tapping of her heels.

The impatient beaks of woodpeckers riveting at the stout mahogany heart of his city. Fluttering taps, light-footed, strong legs and quick feet.

He had then seen the white sweater, a beacon in the distance, coming nearer and nearer, losing its two-dimensionality as it grew closer, expanding until it had the three-sidedness of a work of sculpture, then taking on reality, becoming woolen fiber covering firm high breasts.

He had seen the red hair then, long, lapped by the nervous fingers of the wind, enveloping her head like a blazing funeral pyre. He had stood in the alleyway across the street and watched her as she pranced by, cursing his station, wishing he had posted himself on the other side of the street instead. She carried a black patent-leather sling bag over her shoulder, the strap loose, the bag knocking against her left hipbone as she walked. The bag looked heavy.

He knew that looks could be deceiving, that many women carried all sorts of junk in their purses, but he smelled money in this one. She was either a whore drumming up trade or a society bitch out for a late-evening stroll—it was sometimes difficult to tell them apart. Whichever she was, the purse promised money, and money was what he needed pretty badly right now.

The newspapers shrieking about Jeannie Paige, Jesus!

They had driven him clear off the streets. But how long can a murder remain hot? And doesn't a man have to eat?

He watched the redhead swing past, and then he ducked into the alleyway, quickly calculating a route which would intersect her apparent course.

He did not see Willis coming up behind the girl.

Nor did Willis see him.

There are three lampposts on each block Eileen thought.

It takes approximately one and one-half minutes to cover the distance between lampposts. Four and a half minutes a block. That's plain arithmetic.

Nor is that exceptionally fast. If Willis thinks that's fast, he should meet my brother. My brother is the type of person who rushes through everything—breakfast, dinner . . .

Hold it now!

Something was moving up ahead.

Her mind, as if instantly sucked clean of debris by a huge vacuum cleaner, lay glistening like a hard, cut diamond. Her left hand snapped to the drawstrings on her purse, wedging into the purse and enlarging the opening. She felt the reassuring steel of the .38, content that the butt was in position to be grapsed instantly be a cross-body swipe of her right hand.

She walked with her head erect. She did not break her stride. The figure ahead was a man, of that much she

99

was certain. He had seen her now, and he moved toward her rapidly. He wore a dark-blue suit, and he was hatless. He was a big man, topping six feet.

"Hey!" he called. "Hey, you!" and she felt her heart lurch into her throat because she knew with rattling certainty that this was Clifford.

And suddenly, she felt quite foolish.

She had seen the markings on the sleeve of the blue suit, had seen the slender white lines on the collar. The man she'd thought to be Clifford was only a hatless sailor. The tenseness flooded from her body. A small smile touched her lips.

The sailor came closer to her, and she saw now that he was weaving unsteadily, quite unsteadily. He was, to be kind, as drunk as a lord, and his condition undoubtedly accounted for his missing white hat.

"Wal now," he bawled, "if'n it ain' a redhaid! C'mere, redhaid!"

He grabbed for Eileen, and she knocked his arm aside quickly and efficiently. "Run along, sailor," she said. "You're in the wrong pew!"

The sailor threw back his head and guffawed boisterously. "Th' wrong pew!" he shouted. "Wal now, Ah'll be hung fer a hoss thief!"

Eileen, not caring at all what he was hung for so long as he kept his nose out of the serious business afoot, walked briskly past him and continued on her way.

"Hey!" he bellowed. "Wheah y'goin'?"

She heard his hurried footsteps behind her, and then she felt his hand close on her elbow. She whirled, shaking his fingers free.

"Whutsamatter?" he asked. "Doan'choo like sailors?"

"I like them fine," Eileen answered. "But I think you ought to be getting back to your ship. Now go ahead. Run along." She stared at him levelly.

He returned her stare soberly, and then quite suddenly asked, "Hey, you-all like t'go to bed wi' me?"

Eileen could not suppress the smile. "No," she said. "Thank you very much."

"Why not?" he asked, thrusting forward his jaw.

"I'm married," she lied.

"Why, tha's awright," he said. "Ah'm married, too."

"My husband is a cop," she further lied.

"Cops doan scare me none. On'y the S.O.B.S.P. Ah got to worry 'bout. Hey now, how 'bout it, huh?"

"No," Eileen said firmly. She turned to go, and he wove quickly around her, skidding to a stop in front of her.

"We can talk 'bout yo' husbin an' mah wife, how's that? Ah got the sweetes' li'l wife in th' whole wide world."

"Then go home to her," Eileen said.

"Ah cain't? Damnit all, she's in Alabama!"

"Take off, sailor," Eileen said. "I'm serious. Take off before you get yourself in trouble."

"No," he said, pouting. "Ah wanna go t'bed wi' you."

"Oh, for Pete's sake," she said.

"Ain' nothin' wrong wi' that, is they? Everythin' 'bout it is puffectly normal."

"Except your timing," Eileen said.

"Huh?"

"Nothing." She turned and looked over her shoulder for Willis. He was nowhere in sight. He was undoubtedly resting against an alley wall, laughing his fool head off. She walked around the sailor and started up the street. The sailor fell in beside her.

"Nothin' Ah like better'n walkin'," he said. "Ah'm goan walk mah big feet off, right here 'longside you, till you admit you're just a-dyin' to climb into bed with me. Ah'm goan walk till hell freezes over."

"Stick with me, and you will," Eileen muttered, and then she wondered how soon it would be until she spotted an S.P. Damnit, there never was a cop around when you needed one!

Now she's picking up sailors, Willis thought.

We've got nothing better to do than humor the fleet. Why doesn't she conk the silly son of a bitch on the head and leave him to sleep it off in an alleyway?

How the hell are we going to smoke Clifford if she insists on a naval escort? Shall I go break it up? Or has she got something up her sleeve?

The terrible thing about working with women is that you can never count on them to think like men.

I should have stood in bed.

101

He watched silently, and he cursed the sailor.

Where had the fool materialized from? How could he get that purse now? Of all the goddamn rotten luck, the first good thing that had come along on his first night out since the papers started that Jeannie Paige fuss, and this stupid sailor had to come along and screw it up.

Maybe he'd go away.

Maybe she'd slap him across the face and he'd go away.

Or maybe not. If she was a prostitute, she'd take the sailor with her, and that would be the end of that.

Why did the police allow the Navy to dump its filthy cargoes into the streets of the city, anyway?

He watched the wiggle of the girl's backside, and he watched the swaying, bobbing motion of the sailor, and he cursed the police, and he cursed the fleet, and he even cursed the red-head.

And then they turned the corner, and he ducked through the alley and started through the back yard, hoping to come out some two blocks ahead of the pair, hoping she'd have got rid of him by then, his fingers aching to close around the purse that swung so heavily from her left shoulder.

"What ship are you on?" Eileen asked the sailor.

"U.S.S. Huntuh," the sailor said. "You-all beginnin' t'take an intrust in me, redhaid?"

Eileen stopped. She turned to face the sailor, and there was a deadly glint in her green eyes. "Listen to me, sailor," she said. "I'm a policewoman, understand? I'm working now, and you're cluttering up my job, and I don't like it."

"A *what?*" the sailor said. He threw back his head, ready to let out with a wild guffaw, but Eileen's coldly dispassionate voice stopped him.

"I've got a .38 Detective's Special in my purse," she said evenly. "In about six seconds, I'm going to take it out and shoot you in the leg. I'll leave you on the sidewalk and then put a call in to the Shore Patrol. I'm counting, sailor."

102

"Hey, whut you—"

"One . . ."

"Listen, whut you gettin' all het up about? Ah'm on'y—"

"Two . . ."

"I dont even believe you got an' ol' gun in that—"

The .38 snapped into view suddenly. The sailor's eyes went wide.

"Three," Eileen said.

"Wal, Ah'll be—"

"Four . . ."

The sailor looked at the gun once more.

"G'night, lady," he said, and he turned on his heel and began running. Eileen watched him. She returned the gun to her purse, smiled, turned the corner, and walked into the darkened street. She had taken no more than fifteen steps when the arm circled her throat and she was pulled into the alleyway.

The sailor came down the street at such a fast clip that Willis almost burst out laughing. The flap of the sailor's jumper danced in the wind. He charged down the middle of the asphalt with a curious mixture of a sailor's roll, a drunk's lopsided gait, and the lope of a three-year-old in the Kentucky Derby. His eyes were wide, and his hair flew madly as he jounced along.

He skidded to a stop when he saw Willis and then, puffing for breath, he advised, "Man, if'n you-all see a redhaid up theah, steer clear of her, Ah'm tellin' you."

"What's the matter?" Willis asked paternally, holding back the laugh that crowded his throat.

"Whutsamatter! Man, she got a twenty-guage shotgun in her handbag, tha's whutsamatter. Whoo-ie, Ah'm gettin' clear the hell out o' here!"

He nodded briefly at Willis, and then blasted off again. Willis watched his jet trail, indulged himself in one short chuckle, and then looked for Eileen up ahead. She had probably turned the corner.

He grinned, changing his earlier appraisal of the sailor's intrusion. The sailor had, after all, presented a welcome diversion from this dull business of plodding along and hoping for a mugger who probably would never materialize.

She was reaching for the .38 in her purse when the strap left her shoulder. She felt the secure weight of the purse leaving her hipbone, and then the bag was gone. And just as she planted her feet to throw the intruder over her shoulder, he spun her around and slammed her against the wall of the building.

"I'm not playing around," he said in a low, menacing voice, and she realized instantly that he wasn't. The collision with the wall of the building had knocked the breath out of her. She watched his face, dimly lighted in the alleyway. He was not wearing sunglasses, but she could not determine the color of his eyes. He was wearing a hat, too, and she cursed the hat because it hid his hair.

His fist lashed out suddenly, exploding just beneath her left eye. She had heard about purple and yellow globes of light which followed a punch in th eye, but she had never experienced them until this moment. She tried to move away from the wall, momentarily blinded, but he shoved her back viciously.

"That's just a warning," he said. "Don't scream when I'm gone, you understand?"

"I understand," she said levelly. *Willis, where are you?* her mind shrieked. *For God's sake, where are you?*

She had to detain this man. She had to hold him until Willis showed. Come on, Willis.

"Who are you?" she asked.

His hand went out again, and her head rocked from his strong slap.

"Shut up!" he warned. "I'm taking off now."

If this were Clifford, she had a chance. If this were Clifford, she would have to move in a few seconds, and she tensed herself for the move, knowing only that she had to hold the man until Willis arrived.

There!

He was going into it now.

"Clifford thanks you, madam," he said, and his arm swept across his waist, and he went into a low bow, and Eileen clasped both hands together, raised them high over head, and swung them at the back of his neck as if she were wielding a hammer.

The blow caught him completely by surprise. He began to pitch forward, and she brought up her knee, catching him under the jaw. His arms opened wide. He dropped the purse and staggered backward, and when he lifted his head again Eileen was standing with a spike-heeled shoe in one hand. She didn't wait for his attack. With one foot shoeless, she hobbled forward and swung out at his head.

He backed away, missing her swing, and then he bellowed like a wounded bear, and cut loose with a roundhouse blow that caught her just below her bosom. She felt the sharp knifing pain, and then he was hitting her again, hitting her cruelly and viciously now. She dropped the shoe, and she caught at his clothes, one hand going to his face, trying to rip, try to claw, forgetting all her police knowledge in that one desperate lunge for self-survival, using a woman's weapons—nails.

She missed his face, and she stumbled forward, catching at his jacket again, clawing at the breast pocket. He pulled away, and she felt the material tear, and then she was holding the torn shield of his pocket patch in her hands, and he hit her again, full on the jaw, and she fell back against the wall and heard Willis' running footsteps.

The mugger stooped down for the fallen purse, seizing it by the shoulder straps as Willis burst into the mouth of the alley, a gun in his fist.

Clifford came erect, swinging the bag as he stood. The bag caught Willis on the side of the head, and he staggered sideward, the gun going off in his hand. He shook his head, saw the mugger taking flight, shot without aiming, shot again, missing both times. Clifford turned the corner, and Willis took off after him, rounding the same bend.

The mugger was nowhere in sight.

He went back to where Eileen Burke sat propped against the wall of the building. Her knees were up, and her skirt was pulled back, and she sat in a very unladylike position, cradling her head. Her left eye was beginning to throb painfully. When she lifted her head, Willis winced.

"He clipped you," he said.

"Where the hell were you?" Eileen Burke answered. "Right behind you. I didn't realize anything was

105

wrong until I heard a man's voice shout, 'Shut up!' "

"The son of a bitch packs a wallop," Eileen said. "How does my eye look?"

"You're going to have a hell of a mouse," Willis told her. "We'll get a steak for it whenever you feel like going." He paused. "Was it Clifford?"

"Sure," she said. She got to her feet, and then winced. "Ow, I think he broke one of my ribs."

"Are you kidding me?" Willis asked, concerned.

Eileen felt the area beneath her breasts. "It only feels that way. Oooooh, God!"

"Did you get a look at him?"

"Too dark," she said. She held up her hand. "I got his pocket, though."

"Good." Willis looked down. "What's all this on the sidewalk?"

"What?"

He bent. "Cigarettes," he said. "Good. We may get some latents from the cellophane." He picked the package up with his handkerchief, carefully holding the linen around it.

"He was probably carrying them in his pocket," Eileen said. She touched the throbbing eye. "Let's get that steak, huh?"

"Sure. Just one thing."

"What?"

"Matches. If he was carrying cigarettes in that pocket, he was probably carrying matches, too." He took a pocket flash and thumbed it into life. The light spilled onto the sidewalk, traveling in a slow arc. "Ah, there they are," he said. He stooped to pick up the match folder, using a second handkerchief he took from his inside pocket.

"Listen, can't we get that steak?" Eileen asked.

Willis looked at the folder. "We may be in luck," he said.

"How so?"

"The ad on these matches. It's for a place here in the city. A place named the Three Aces. Maybe we've got a hangout for Clifford now."

He looked at Eileen and grinned broadly. She stooped, put on her shoe.

"Come on," he said, "let's take care of that peeper."

"I was beginning to think you didn't care any more," Eileen said. She took his arm, and they started up the street together.

13

That Thursday afternoon, Kling called Claire Townsend the first chance he got.

The first chance he got was on his lunch hour. He ordered a Western sandwich and a cup of coffee, went to the phone-book looked up Townsend at 728 Peterson in Riverhead, and came up with a listing for Ralph Townsend. He went into the booth, deposited a dime, and dialed the number. He allowed the phone to ring for a total of twelve times, and then he hung up.

There were a lot of things to keep him busy on the beat that afternoon. A woman, for no apparent reason other than that her husband had called her "Babe," had struck out at him with a razor, opening a gash the size of a banana on the side of his face. Kling made the pinch. The razor, by the time he had arrived on the scene, had gone the way of all discreet assault weapons —down the nearest sewer.

No sooner was he back on the street than a gang of kids attacked a boy as he was coming home from school. The boy had committed the unpardonable sin of making a pass at a deb who belonged to a rival street gang. Kling arrived just as the gang members were ready to stomp the kid into the pavement. He collared one of them, told him he knew the faces of all the kids who'd participated in the beating, and that if anything happened to the boy they'd jumped from here on in, he'd know just where to look. The gang member nodded solemnly, and then took off after his friends. The boy they'd jumped survived with only a few bumps on his head. This time, fists had been the order of the day.

Kling then proceeded to break up a crap game in the hallway of one of the buildings, listen to the ranting complaints of a shopkeeper who insisted that an eight-year-old boy had swiped a bolt of blue Shantung, warn one of the bar owners that his license was kaput the next

107

time any hustlers were observed soliciting in his joint, have a cup of coffee with one of the better-known policy runners in the neighborhood, and then walk back to the precinct house, where he changed into street clothes.

As soon as he hit the street again, he called Claire. She picked up the instrument on the fourth ring.

"Who is it?" she said, "and I hope to hell you apologize for getting me out of the shower. I'm wringing wet."

"I apologize," Kling said.

"Mr. Kling?" she asked, recognizing his voice.

"Yes."

"I was going to call you, but I didn't know where. I remembered something that might help."

"What is it?"

"The night I walked Jeannie down to the train station she said something."

"What?"

"She said she had a half-hour ride ahead of her. Does that help?"

"It might. Thanks a lot." He paused. "Listen, I've been thinking."

"Yes."

"About . . . about this dinner setup. I thought maybe—"

"Mr. Kling," she interrupted, "you don't want to take me to dinner."

"I do," he insisted.

"I'm the dullest girl in the world, believe me. I'd bore you stiff."

"I'd like to take the chance."

"You're only asking for trouble for yourself. Don't bother, believe me. Buy your mother a present with the money."

"I bought my mother a present last week."

"Buy her another one."

"Besides, I was thinking of going Dutch."

Claire chuckled. "Well, now you make it sound more attractive."

"Seriously, Claire—"

"Seriously, Mr. Kling, I'd rather not. I'm a sad sack, and you wouldn't enjoy me, one bit."

"I enjoy you already."

"Those were company manners."

"Say, have you got an inferiority complex or something?"

"It's not that I have an inferiority complex, doctor," she said, "it's that I really *am* inferior." Kling laughed, and she said, "Do you remember that cartoon?"

"No, but it's wonderful. How about dinner?"

"Why?"

"I like you."

"There are a million girls in this city."

"More than that even."

"Mr. Kling—"

"Bert."

"Bert, there's nothing here for you."

"I haven't said what I want yet."

"Whatever you want, it's not here."

"Claire, let me gamble on it. Let me take you to dinner, and let me spend what may turn out to be the most miserable evening in my entire life. I've gambled with larger stakes involved. In the service, I even gambled with my life once in a while."

"Were you in the service?" she asked.

"Yes."

There seemed to be sudden interest in her voice. "Korea?"

"Yes."

There was a long silence on the line.

"Claire?"

"I'm here."

"What's the matter?"

"Nothing."

"Deposit five cents for the next three minutes, please," the operator said.

"Oh, hell, just a minute," Kling replied. He dug into his pocket and deposited a nickel. "Claire?" he said.

"I'm costing you money already," she told him.

"I've got money to burn," he answered. "How about it? I'll call for you tonight at about six-thirty."

"No, tonight is out of the question."

"Tomorrow night then."

"I have a late class tomorrow. I don't get out until seven."

"I'll meet you at the school."

"That won't give me any time to change."

"It'll be a come-as-you-are date, okay?"

"I usually wear flats and a dirty old sweater to school."

"Fine!" he said enthusiastically.

"I suppose I could wear a dress and heels, though. It might shock some of the slobs in our hallowed halls, but then again it might set a precedent."

"Seven o'clock?"

"All right," she said.

"Good, I'll see you then."

"Good-by."

" 'By." He hung up, grinning. He was stepping out of the booth when he remembered. Instantly, he reached into his pocket for another dime. He had no change. He went to the proprietor of the candy store, who was busy doling out a couple of two-cent seltzers. By the time he got his change, five minutes had rushed by. He dialed the number rapidly.

"Hello?"

"Claire, this is me again."

"You got me out of the shower again, you know that, don't you?"

"Gee, I'm awfully sorry, but you didn't tell me *which* school."

"Oh." Claire was silent. "Nope, I didn't. It's Women's U. Do you know where that is?"

"Yes."

"Fine. Go to Radley Hall. You'll find the office of our alleged college newspaper there. The paper is called *The Radley Clarion,* but the sign on the door says *The Radley Rag.* I keep my coat in a locker there. Don't let all the predatory females frighten you."

"I'll be there on the dot," Kling said.

"And I, exercising a woman's prerogative, shall be there ten minutes *after* the dot."

"I'll wait."

"Good. Now you don't mind, do you, but I'm making a big puddle on the carpet."

"I'm sorry. Go wash."

"You said that as if you thought I was dirty."

"If you'd rather talk, I've got all night."

"I'd rather wash. Good-by, Tenacious."

"Good-by, Claire."

"You *are* tenacious, you realize that, don't you?"

Kling grinned. "Tenacious, anyone?" he asked.

"Ouch!" Claire said. "Good-by," and then she hung up.

He sat in the booth grinning foolishly for a good three minutes. A fat lady finally knocked on the glass panel in the door and said, "Young man, that booth isn't a hotel."

Kling opened the doors. "That's funny," he said. "Room service just sent up a sandwich."

The woman blinked, pulled a face, and then stuffed herself into the booth, slamming the door emphatically.

At ten o'clock that night, Kling stepped off an express train onto the Peterson Avenue station platform of the Elevated Transit System. He stood for a moment looking out over the lights of the city, warm and alive with color against the tingling autumn air. Autumn did not want to die this year. Autumn refused to be lowered into the grave of winter. She clung tenaciously ("Tenacious, anyone?" he thought, and he grinned all over again) to the trailing robes of summer. She was glad to be alive, and humanity caught some of her zest for living, mirrored it on the faces of the people in the streets.

One of the people in the streets was a man named Clifford.

Somewhere among people who rushed along grinning, there was a man with a scowl on his face.

Somewhere among the thousands who sat in movie houses, there might be a murderer watching the screen.

Somewhere where lovers walked and talked, he might be sitting alone on a bench, brooding.

Somewhere where open, smiling faces dispelled plumed, brittle vapor onto the snappish air, a man walked with his mouth closed and his teeth clenched.

Clifford.

How many Cliffords were there in a city of this size? How many Cliffords in the telephone directory? How many unlisted Cliffords?

Shuffle the deck of Cliffords, cut, and then pick a Clifford, any Clifford.

This was not a time for picking Cliffords.

This was a time for walks in the country, with the air spanking your cheeks, and the leaves crisp and crunching underfoot, and the trees screaming in a riot of splendid color. This was a time for brier pipes and tweed overcoats and juicy red McIntosh apples. This was a time to contemplate pumpkin pie and good books and thick rugs and windows shut tight against the coming cold.

This was not a time for Clifford, and this was not a time for murder.

But murder had been done, and the Homicide cops were cold-eyed men who had never been seventeen.

Kling had once been seventeen.

He walked down the steps and directly to the change booth. The man behind the grilled window was reading a "comic" book. Kling recognized it as one of the more hilarious attempts now on the stands, a strip dealing with a widow who had multiple sclerosis. The attendant looked up.

"Good evening," Kling said.

The attendant eyed him suspiciously. "Evening," he replied.

"Mind if I ask you a few questions?"

"Depends what the questions are," the attendant said.

"Well—"

"If you're planning a holdup, young man, forget it," the attendant advised. "You won't get a hell of a lot for your trouble, and the cops in this town are pretty damn good on transit stickups."

"Thanks. I wasn't planning a holdup."

"Good thing. My name's Ruth, Sam Ruth. The fellows call this 'Ruth's Booth.' What can I do for you?"

"Are you usually working nights?"

"Sometimes yes, sometimes no. Why?"

"I'm trying to trace a young girl who generally boarded a train from this platform."

"Lots of young girls get on trains here."

"This one usually came up between ten and ten-thirty. Are you on at that time?"

"When I work the afternoon shift, I come on at four, and I go off at midnight."

"Then you're on at ten."

"It would appear that way, yeah."

"This girl was a blonde," Kling said. "A very pretty blonde."

112

"There's a blond widow works in the bakeshop downstairs. She comes up about eight each night."

"This girl was young. Seventeen."

"Seventeen, huh?"

"Yes."

"Don't recall," Ruth said.

"Think."

"What for? I don't recall her."

"Very pretty. If you'd seen her, you'd remember her. Well built, big blue eyes, a knockout."

Ruth squinched up his eyes. "Yeah," he said.

"Huh?"

"I remember. Nice young kid. Yeah, I remember."

"What time did she come up?"

"'Bout ten-twenty-five usually. Yeah, I remember her, all right. Always went up the downtown side of the platform. Used to watch her all the way. A damn pretty girl. Only seventeen, you say? Seemed a lot older."

"Only seventeen. Are you sure we're talking about the same girl?"

"Listen, how do I know? This blonde came up about ten-twenty-five most of the time. Reason I remember her is she once asked me to change a ten-dollar bill. We ain't allowed to change bigger than two dollars, not that many folks carry two-dollar bills, you know. Consider it hard luck. Superstition's bad, bad." Ruth shook his head.

"Did you change it for her?" Kling asked.

"Out of my own pocket. That's how I remember her. She gave me a big smile. Nice smile, that girl. Nice everything, you ask me. Yeah, she's the one, all right. Used to go up on the downtown side, caught the ten-thirty train." Ruth pulled a gold watch from his pocket. He nodded, replaced the watch. "Yeah, caught the ten-thirty."

"All the time?"

"Whenever I seen her, she caught the same train. After I cashed that bill for her, she always give me a smile. She was worth looking at, all right. Biggest damn boobies I ever seen on a woman."

Kling glanced over his sholder. The clock on the wall read 10:16.

113

"If I got on that ten-thirty train," he asked, "where would I get off a half hour from now?"

"Say, I don't know," Ruth said. He thought for a moment. "Can tell you how to find out, though."

"Yes?"

"Get on it," Ruth said.

"Thanks."

"Not at all. Glad to be of help." He turned back to his comic book, anxious to get back to the funny pages about the sick widow.

The train screeched through the heart of the city, on intimate terms with the windows of the buildings it passed. Kling sat and watched the city pass by in review outside. It was a big city, and a dirty city, but when you were born and raised in it, it became as much a part of you as your liver or your intestinal tract. He watched the city, and he watched the hands of his timepiece.

Jeannie Paige had told Claire there was a half-hour ride ahead of her. She had generally boarded a ten-thirty train and so Kling watched the advancing hands of his watch. The train swooped underground, piercing the bowels of the city. He sat and waited. Passengers came and went. Kling's eyes did not leave his watch.

At 11:02, the train pulled into a station platform underground. The last stop had been at 10:58. It was a tossup, either way. He left the train and went up to the street.

He was in the heart of Isola.

The buildings reached up to touch the sky, tinting the night with gaudy smears of red and orange and green and yellow light. There was a men's clothing store on the corner, and a bakery shop, and a hack stand, and a dress shop, and a bus stop up the street, and a movie marquee, and a candy store, and a Chinese restaurant, and a bar, and all the stores and signs that clustered together like close relatives of the same family all over the city.

He sighed heavily.

If Jeannie had met her boy-friend here, and if her boy-friend's name was Clifford, combing the area would be like searching for a blade of hay in a mountain of needles.

He went to the subway kiosk again, boarding an uptown train this time. He traveled for one stop, figuring the half hour Jeannie had estimated could just as easily have brought her to this station.

The stores and signs he encountered on the street were much the same as those he had just seen. The trappings of a busy intersection. Hell, this stop was almost a dead ringer for the one he'd just visited.

Almost—but not quite.

Kling boarded the train again and headed for his furnished room.

There had been one landmark at the first stop which had been missing at the second stop. Kling's eyes had recorded the item on his brain and buried it in his unconscious.

Unfortunately, however, it was useless there at the moment.

14

Science, as any fool knows, is the master sleuth.

Give the Police Lab a sliver of glass and they can tell you what make car the suspect was driving, when he last had it washed, what states he'd visited, and whether or not he'd ever necked in the back seat.

Provided the breaks are with them.

When the breaks are going the wrong way, science is about as master a sleuth as the corner iceman.

The breaks in the Jeannie Paige case managed to show a total disregard for the wishes and earnest endeavors of the boys in the Police Laboratory. There had, in all truth, been a good thumbprint on one lens of the sunglasses found near the girl's body. Unfortunately, it is about as difficult to trace a single print as it is to unmask a Moslem woman. This did not faze the boys in the lab.

Sam Grossman was a lab technician and a police lieutenant.

He was tall and thin, a gentle man with gentle eyes and a quiet manner. He wore glasses, the only sign of science on a rock-hewn face that seemed to have been dispossessed from a New England farm. He worked at Headquarters in the clean, white lab that stretched across half the first-floor length of the building. He liked police work. He owned an orderly, precise mind, and there was something neat and truthful about the coupling of indisputable scientific fact to police theory.

He was an emotional man, but he had long ago ceased identifying the facts of sudden death with the people it summarily visited. He had seen too many bundles of bloody clothing, had studied the edges of too many powder burns, had analyzed the liquid contents of too many poisoned stomachs. Death, to Sam Grossman, was the great equalizer. It reduced human beings to arithmetical problems. If the breaks went with the lab, two and two added up to four.

If the breaks were indifferent or downright ornery, two and two sometimes equaled five, or six, or eleven.

There had been a man at the scene of Jeannie Paige's death. The man had been equipped with a soft-pine sketchboard attached to a photographic tripod. He had also carried a small alidade, a compass, graph paper, a soft-lead pencil, India rubber, common pins, a wooden triangle with scale, a scale, a tape measure, and a flexible steel ruler.

The man had worked quietly and efficiently. While photographers swarmed over the site, while technicians dusted for latent prints, while the position of the body was marked and while the body was transported into the waiting meat wagon, while the area was carefully scrutinized for footprints or tire tracks—the man stood like an artist doing a picture of a farmer's barn on Cape Cod.

He said Hello to the detectives who occasionally stopped to chat with him. He seemed unmindful of the activity which erupted everywhere around him.

Quietly, efficiently, carefully, methodically, he sketched the scene of the crime. Then he packed up and went to his office, where, working from the preliminary sketch, he made a more detailed drawing. The drawing was printed up and, together with the detailed photos taken at the site, sent to the many departments interested in solving the mugger murder.

Sam Grossman's interest was definitely turned in that

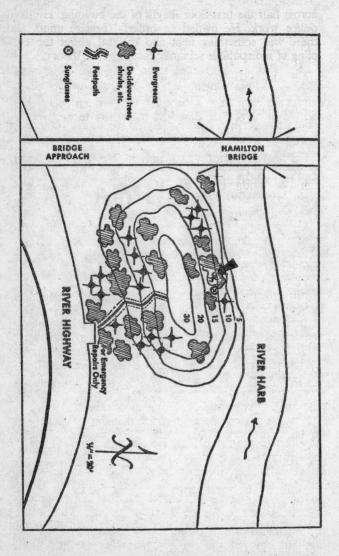

BRIDGE
APPROACH

HAMILTON
BRIDGE

RIVER HIGHWAY

RIVER HARB

For Emergency
Repairs Only

Evergreens

Deciduous trees,
shrubs, etc.

Footpath

Sunglasses

5
10
15
20
30

¼" = 20'

direction, and so a copy of the drawing reached his desk. Since color or the lack of color played no important part in this particular homicide, the drawing was in black and white.

Grossman studied it with the dispassionate scrutiny an art dealer gives a potentially fake van Gogh.

The girl had been found at the base of a fifteen-foot drop, one of the shelf-like levels which sloped down in a cliff to the river bed. A footpath led through evergreens and maples from an Emergency Repairs turnoff to the highest point of the cliff, some thirty feet above the River Harb.

The Repairs cutoff was plainly visible from the River Highway, which swung around in a wide arc under the Hamilton Bridge approach. The footpath, however, was screened from the highway by trees and shrubs, as were the actual sloping sides of the cliff itself.

A good set of tire tracks had been found in a thin layer of earth caked on the River side of the Repairs cutoff. A pair of sunglasses had been found alongside the dead girl's body.

That was all.

Unfortunately, the sides of the cliff sloped upward in igneous formidability. The path wound its way over solid prehistoric rock. Neither the girl nor her murderer had left any footprints for the lab boys to play with.

Unfortunately, too, though the path was screened by bushes and trees, none of the plant life encroached upon the path's right to meander to the top of the cliff. In short, there was no fabric, leather, feathers, or telltale dust caught upon twigs or resting upon leaves.

It was a reasonable assumption that the girl had been driven to the spot of her death. There were no signs of any repairs having been made in the cutoff. If the auto had pulled in with a flat tire, the jack would have left marks on the pavement, and the tools might have left grease stains or metal scrapings. There was the possibility, of course, that the car had suffered an engine failure, in which case the hood would have been lifted and the mechanism studied. But the caked earth spread in an arc that covered the corners and sides of the cutoff. Anyone standing at the front of the car to lift the hood

118

would surely have left footprints. There were none, nor were there any signs of prints having been brushed away.

The police assumed, therefore, that the girl and her murderer had been driving west on the River Highway, had pulled into the Emergency Repairs cutoff, and had then proceeded on foot to the top of the cliff.

The girl had been killed at the top of the cliff.

She had been alive up to then. There were no bloodstains along the path leading upward. With a head wound such as she had suffered, her blood would have soaked the rocks on the path if she had been killed earlier and then carried from the car.

The instrument used to split her skull and her face had been heavy and blunt. The girl had undoubtedly reached for her killer's face, snatching off the sunglasses. She had then gone over the cliff, and the sunglasses had left her hand.

It would have been easy to assume that the lens of the glasses had shattered upon contact with the ground. This was not the case. The technicians could find not a scrap, not a sliver of glass on the ground. The sunglasses, then, had been shattered before they went over the side of the cliff. Nor had they been shattered anywhere in the area. The lab boys searched in vain for glass. The notion of a man wearing sunglasses with one ruptured lens was a curious one, but the facts stood.

The sunglasses, of course, had drawn a blank. Five-and-dime stuff.

The tire tracks had seemed promising at first. But when the cast was studied and comparison data checked, the tires on the car proved to be as helpful as the sunglasses had been.

The tire size was 6.70-15.

The tire weight was twenty-three pounds.

The tire was made of rubber reinforced with nylon cord, the thread design featuring hook "sipes" to block skids and side-slip.

The tire retailed for $18.04, including Federal tax.

The tire could be had by any man jack in the U.S. of A. who owned a Sears, Roebuck catalogue. The trade name of the tire was "Allstate."

You could order one or a hundred and one by sending your dough and asking for catalogue number 95N03067K.

There were probably eighty thousand people in the city who had four of the tires on each of their cars, not to mention a spare in the trunk.

The tire tracks told Grossman one thing: The car that had pulled into the cutoff was a light car. The tire size and weight eliminated any of the heavier cars on the road.

Grossman felt like a man who was all dressed up with no place to go.

Resignedly, he turned to the pocket patch Eileen Burke had ripped from the mugger's jacket.

When Roger Havilland stopped by for the test results that Friday afternoon, Grossman said the patch was composed of 100 percent nylon and that it belonged to a suit which retailed for $32.00 in a men's clothing chain. The chain had sixty-four stores spread throughout the city. The suit came in only one color: blue.

Havilland gravely considered the impossibility of getting any lead from a suit sold in sixty-four stores. He scratched his head in misery.

And then he said, "Nylon? Who the hell wears nylon in the fall?"

Meyer Meyer was exuberant.

He burst into the Squad Room, and he waltzed over to where Temple was fishing in the file, and he slapped his partner on the back.

"They cracked it!" he shouted.

"What?" Temple said. "Jesus, Meyer, you damn near cracked my back. What the hell are you talking about?"

"The cats," Meyer said, shrewdly studying Temple.

"What cats?"

"The 33rd Precinct. This guy who was going around kidnaping cats. Jesus Christ, I tell you this is the eeriest case they've ever cracked. I was talking to Agnucci, do you know him? He's 3rd/Grade down there, been working on this one all along, handled most of the squeals. Well, man, they've cracked it." Meyer studied Temple patiently.

"So what'd it turn out to be?" Temple asked, his interest piqued.

"They got their first lead the other night," Meyer said. "They got a squeal from some woman who said an Angora had been swiped. Well, they came upon this guy in an alleyway, and guess what he was doing?"

"What?" Temple asked.

"Burning the cat!"

"Burning the cat? You mean, setting fire to the cat?"

"Yep," Meyer said, nodding. "He stopped when they showed, and he ran like hell. They saved the cat, and they also got a good description of the suspect. After that, it was duck soup."

"When'd they get him?" Temple asked.

"This afternoon. They broke into his apartment, and it was the damnedest thing ever, I'm telling you. This guy was actually burning up the cats, burning them to this powdery ash."

"I don't believe it," Temple said.

"So help me. He'd kidnap the cats and burn them into ashes. He had shelves and shelves of these little jars, full of cat ashes."

"But what in holy hell for?" Temple asked. "Was the guy nuts?"

"Nossir," Meyer said. "But you can bet the boys at the 33rd were asking the same question."

"Well, what was it?"

"They asked him, George. They asked him just that. Agnucci took him aside and said, 'Listen, Mac, are you nuts or something? What's the idea burnin' up all them cats and then puttin' the ashes in jars like that?' Agnucci asked, all right."

"Well, what'd the guy say?"

Meyer patiently said, "Just what you'd expect him to say. He explained that he wasn't crazy, and that there was a good reason for those cat ashes in all those jars. He explained that he was making something."

"What?" Temple asked anxiously. "What in hell was he making?"

"Instant pussy," Meyer said softly, and then he began chuckling.

15

The report on the package of Pall Mall cigarettes and the match folder came in later that afternoon. It simply stated that each article, as such articles are wont to be, had been fingered a good many times. The only thing the fingerprint boys got from either of them was an overlay of smeared, worthless latents.

The match folder, with its blatant advertisement for the Three Aces was turned over to the Detective Bureau, and the detectives of Homicide North and the 87th Precinct sighed heavily because the match folder meant more goddamned legwork.

Kling dressed for his date carefully.

He didn't know exactly why, but he felt that extreme care should be exercised in the handling and feeding of Claire Townsend. He admitted to himself that he had never—well, hardly ever—been so taken with a girl, and that he would probably be devastated forever—well, for a long time—if he lost her. He had no ideas on exactly how to win her, except for this intuition which urged him to proceed with caution. She had, after all, warned him repeatedly. She had put out the KEEP OFF! sign, and then she had read the sign aloud to him, and then she had translated it into six languages, but she had nonetheless accepted his offer.

Which proves beyond doubt, he thought, *that the girl is wildly in love with me.*

Which piece of deduction was about on a par with the high level of detective work he had done so far. His abortive attempts at getting anywhere with the Jeannie Paige murder left him feeling a little foolish. He wanted very much to be promoted to Detective 3rd/Grade someday, but he entertained severe doubts now as to whether he really was detective material. It was almost two weeks since Peter Bell had come to him with his plea. It was almost two weeks since Bell had scribbled his address on a scrap of paper, a scrap still tucked in one of the pockets of Kling's wallet. A lot had happened in those nearly two weeks. And those happenings gave Kling reason for a little healthy soul-searching.

He was, at this point, just about ready to leave the case to the men who knew how to handle such things. His amateurish legwork, his fumbling questions, had netted a big zero—or so he thought. The only important thing he'd turned up was Claire Townsend. Claire, he was certain, was important. She was important now, and he felt she would become more important as time went by.

So let's polish our goddamn shoes. You want to look like a slob?

He took his shoes from the closet, slipped them on over socks he would most certainly smear with polish and later change, and set to work with his shine kit.

He was spitting on his right shoe when the knock sounded on the door.

"Who is it?" he called.

"Police. Open up," the voice said.

"Who?"

"Police."

Kling rose, his trouser cuffs rolled up high, his hands smeared with black polish. "Is this a gag?" he said to the closed door.

"Come on, Kling," the voice said. "You know better than that."

Kling opened the door. Two men stood in the hallway. Both were huge, both wore tweed jackets over V-necked sweaters, both looked bored.

"Bert Kling?" one of them asked.

"Yes?" he said puzzled.

A shield flashed. "Monoghan and Monroe," one of them said. "Homicide. I'm Monoghan."

"I'm Monroe," the other one said.

They were like Tweedledum and Tweedledee, Kling thought. He suppressed his smile. Neither of his visitors was smiling. Each looked as if he had just come from an out-of-town funeral.

"Come in, fellers," Kling said. "I was just dressing."

"Thank you," Monoghan said.

"Thank you," Monroe echoed.

They stepped into the room. They both took off their

fedoras. Monoghan cleared his throat. Kling looked at them expectantly.

"Like a drink?" he asked, wondering why they were here, feeling somehow awed and frightened by their presence.

"A short one," Monoghan said.

"A tiny hooker," Monroe said.

Kling went to the closet and pulled out a bottle. "Bourbon okay?"

"When I was a patrolman," Monoghan said, "I couldn't afford bourbon."

"This was a gift," Kling said.

"I never took whisky. Anybody on the beat wanted to see me, it was cash on the line."

"That's the only way," Monroe said.

"This was a gift from my father. When I was in the hospital. The nurses wouldn't let me touch it there."

"You can't blame them," Monoghan said.

"Turn the place into an alcoholic ward," Monroe said, unsmiling.

Kling brought them their drinks. Monoghan hesitated. "Ain't you drinking with us?"

"I've got an important date," he said. "I want to keep my head."

Monoghan looked at him with the flat look of a reptile. He shrugged, then turned to Monroe and said, "Here's looking at you."

Monroe acknowledged the toast. "Up yours," he said unsmilingly and then tossed off the shot.

"Good bourbon," Monoghan said.

"Excellent," Monroe amplified.

"More?" Kling asked.

"Thanks," Monoghan said.

"No," Monroe said.

Kling looked at them. "You said you were from homicide?"

"Homicide North."

"Monoghan and Monroe," Monroe said. "Ain't you heard of us? We cracked the Nelson-Nichols-Permen triangle murder."

"Oh," Kling said.

"Sure," Monoghan said modestly. "Big case."

"One of our biggest," Monroe said.

"Big one."

"Yeah."

"What are you working on now?" Kling asked, smiling.

"The Jeannie Paige murder," Monoghan said flatly.

A dart of fear shot up into Kling's throat. "Oh?" he said.

"Yeah," Monoghan said.

"Yeah," Monroe said.

Monoghan cleared his throat. "How long you been with the force, Kling?" he asked.

"Just—Just a short while."

"That figures," Monoghan said.

"Sure," Monroe said.

"You like your job?"

"Yes," Kling answered hesitantly.

"You want to keep it?"

"You want to go on being a cop?"

"Yes, of course."

"Then keep your ass out of Homicide."

"What?" Kling said.

"He means," Monroe explained, "keep your ass out of Homicide."

"I—I don't know what you mean."

"We mean keep away from stiffs. Stiffs are *our* business."

"We like stiffs," Monroe said.

"We're specialists, you understand? You call in a heart doctor when you got heart disease, don't you? You call in an eye, ear, nose and throat man when you got laryngitis, don't you? Okay, when you got a stiff, you call in Homicide. That's us. Monoghan and Monroe."

"You don't call in a wet-pants patrolman."

"Homicide. Not a beat-walker."

"Not a pavement-pounder."

"Not *you!*" Monoghan said.

"Not a night-stick-twirler."

"Not a traffic jockey."

"Clear?" Monroe asked.

"Yes," Kling said.

"Its gonna get a lot clearer," Monoghan added. "The lieutenant wants to see you."

"What for?"

"The lieutenant is a funny guy. He thinks Homicide is the best damn department in the city. He runs Homicide, and he don't like people coming in where they ain't asked. I'll let you in on a secret. He don't even like the *detectives* from your precinct to go messing around in murder. Trouble is, he can't refuse their assistance or their cooperation, specially when your precinct manages to stack up so many goddamn homicides each year. So he suffers the dicks—but he don't have to suffer no goddamn patrolman."

"But—but why does he want to see me? I understand now. I shouldn't have stuck my nose in, and I'm sorry I—"

"You shouldn't have stuck your nose in," Monoghan agreed.

"You definitely shouldn't have."

"But I didn't do any harm. I just—"

"Who knows what harm you done?" Monoghan said.

"You may have done untold harm," Monroe said.

"Ah, hell," Kling said, "I've got a date."

"Yeah," Monoghan said. "With the lieutenant."

"Call your broad," Monroe advised. "Tell her the police are bugging you."

Kling looked at his watch. "I can't reach her," he said. "She's at school."

"Impairing the morals of a minor," Monoghan said, smiling.

"Better you shouldn't mention that to the lieutenant."

"She's in *college*," Kling said. "Listen, will I be through by seven?"

"Maybe," Monoghan said.

"Get your coat," Monroe said.

"He don't need a coat. It's nice and mild."

"It may get chilly later. This is pneumonia weather." Kling sighed heavily. "All right if I wash my hands?"

"What?" Monoghan asked.

"He's polite," Monroe said. He has to take a leak."

"No, I have to wash my hands."

"Okay, so wash them. Hurry up. The lieutenant don't like to be kept waiting."

The building that housed Homicide North was the shabbiest, dowdiest, dirtiest, crummiest building Kling had ever seen. It was a choice spot for Homicide, Kling thought instantly. It even stinks of death. He had followed Monoghan and Monroe past the desk sergeant and then through a narrow, dimly lighted hallway lined with benches. He could hear typewriters clacking behind closed doors. An occasional open door revealed a man in shirt sleeves and shoulder holster. The entire place gave the impression of being the busy office of a numbers banker. Phones rang, people carried files from one office to another, men stopped at the water cooler—all in a dimly illuminated Dante interior.

"Sit down," Monoghan had said.

"Cool your heels a little," Monroe added.

"The lieutenant is dictating a memo. He'll be with you in a little while."

Whatever the good lieutenant was dictating, Kling decided after waiting an hour, it was not a memo. It was probably volume two of his autobiography: *The Patrolman Years.* He had long ago given up the possibility of being on time for his date with Claire. It was now 6:45, and *tempus* was *fugiting* along at a merry clip. With luck, though, he might still catch her at the school, assuming she'd give him the benefit of the doubt and wait around a while. Which, considering her reluctance to make the date in the first place, was a hell of a lot to assume.

Impatiently, Kling bided his time.

At 8:20, he stopped a man in the corridor and asked if he could use a phone. The man studied him sourly and said, "Better wait until after the lieutenant sees you. He's dictating a memo."

"On what?" Kling cracked. "How to dismantle a radio motor-patrol car?"

"What?" the man said. "Oh, I get it. Pretty funny." He left Kling and went to the water cooler. "You want some water?"

"I haven't eaten since noon," Kling said.

"Take a little water. Settle your stomach."

"No bread to go with it?" Kling asked.

"What?" the man said. "Oh, I get it. Pretty funny."

"How much longer do you think he'll be?"

"Depends. He dictates slow."

"How long has he been with Homicide North?"

"Five, ten years. I don't know."

"Where'd he work before this? Dachau?"

"What?" the man said. "Oh, I get it."

"Pretty funny," Kling said dryly. "Where are Monoghan and Monroe?"

"They went home. They're hard workers, those two. Put in a big day."

"Listen," Kling said, "I'm hungry. Can't you kind of goose him a little?"

"The lieutenant?" the man said. "*Me* goose the lieutenant? Jesus, that's the funniest thing you said yet." He shook his head and walked off down the corridor, turning once to look back at Kling increduously.

At 10:33, a detective with a .38 tucked into his waistband came into the corridor.

"Bert Kling?" he asked.

"Yes," Kling said wearily.

"Lieutenant Hawthorne will see you now," he said.

"Glory hall—"

"Don't make wisecracks with the lieutenant," the detective advised. He ain't eaten since suppertime."

He led Kling to a frosted door appropriately marked LIEUTENANT HENRY HAWTHORNE, threw it open, said, "Kling, Lieutenant," and then ushered Kling into the room. The detective left, closing the door behind him.

Hawthorne sat behind a desk at the far end of the room. He was a small man with a bald head and bright blue eyes. The sleeves on his white shirt were rolled up past the elbows. The collar was unbuttoned, the tie knot yanked down. He wore a shoulder holster from which protruded the walnut stock of a .45 automatic. His desk was clean and bare. Green file cabinets formed a fortress wall behind the desk and on the side of it. The blinds on the window to the left of the desk were pulled tightly closed. A wooden plaque on the desk read: LT. HAWTHORNE.

"Kling?" he said. His voice was high and brassy, like a double C forced from the bell of a broken trumpet.

"Yes, sir," Kling said.

"Sit down," Hawthorne said, indicating the straight-backed chair alongside of the desk.

"Thank you, sir," Kling said. He walked to the chair and sat. He was nervous, very nervous. He certainly didn't want to lose his job, and Hawthorne seemed like

128

a tough customer. He wondered if a lieutenant in Homicide could ask the commisioner to fire a patrolman, and he decided a lieutenant in Homicide definitely could. He swallowed. He wasn't thinking of Claire any longer, nor was he thinking of food.

"So you're Mr. Sherlock Holmes, eh?" Hawthorne said.

Kling didn't know what to answer. He didn't know whether to smile or cast his eyes downward. He didn't know whether to sit or go blind.

Hawthone watched him. Emphatically, he repeated, "So you're Mr. Sherlock Holmes, eh?"

"Sir?" Kling said politely.

"Diddling around with a murder case, eh?"

"I didn't realize, sir, that—"

"Listen to me, Sherlock," Hawthorne said, slamming his open palm onto the desk. "We got a phone call here this afternoon." He opened the top drawer. "Clocked in at"—he consulted a pad—"sixteen thirty-seven. Said you were farting around with this Jeannie Paige thing." Hawthorne crashed the desk drawer shut. "I've been very kind to you, Sherlock. I could have gone straight to Captain Frick at the 87th. The 87th happens to be your precinct, and Captain Frick happens to be an old and dear friend of mine, and Captain Frick doesn't take crap from runny-nosed patrolmen who happen to be walking beats. Lieutenant Byrnes of your precinct likes to stick his nose in murder cases, too, and I can't do a hell of alot about that, except occasionally show him I don't too much appreciate his goddamn Aunt Suzianna help! But if the 87th thinks it's going to run in a patrolman on me, if the 87th thinks—"

"Sir, the precinct didn't know anything about my—"

"AND THEY STILL DON'T KNOW!" Hawthorne shouted. "And they don't know because I was kind enough not to mention this to Captain Frick. I'm being good to you, Sherlock, remember that. I'm being goddamn good and kind to you, so don't give me any crap!"

"Sir, I wasn't—"

"All right, listen to me, Sherlock. If I hear again that you're even *thinking* about Jeannie Paige, your ass is going to be in one big sling. I'm not talking about a transfer to a beat in Bethtown, either. I'm talking about

OUT! You are going to be out in the street. You are going to be out and cold. And don't think I can't do it."

"Sir, I didn't think—"

"I know the commissioner the way I know the back of my own hand. The commissioner would sell his wife if I asked him to, that's the way I know the commissioner. So don't for one second think the commissioner wouldn't toss a snot-nosed patrolman right out on his ear if I asked him to. Don't for one minute think that, Sherlock."

"Sir—"

"And don't for a minute think I'm kidding, Sherlock, because I never kid around where it concerns murder. You're fooling with murder, do you realize that? You've been barging around asking questions, and Christ alone knows who you've scared into hiding, and Christ alone knows how much of our careful work you've fouled up! SO LAY OFF! Go walk your goddamn beat! If I get another squeal about you—"

"Sir?"

"WHAT IS IT?"

"Who called you, sir?"

"That's none of your goddamn business!" Hawthorne shouted.

"Yes, sir."

"Get out of my office. Jesus, you make me sick. Get out of my office."

"Yes, sir," Kling said. He turned and went to the door.

"AND DON'T FOOL WITH MURDER!" Hawthorne shouted after him.

He called Claire at 11:10. The phone rang six times, and he was ready to hang up, afraid he'd caught her asleep, when the receiver was lifted.

"Hello?" she said. Her voice was sleepy.

"Claire?"

"Yes, who's this?"

"Did I wake you?"

"Yes." There was a pause, and then her voice became a bit more lively. "Bert? Is that you?"

"Yes. Claire, I'm sorry I—"

130

"The last time I got stood up was when I was sixteen and had a—"

"Claire, I didn't stand you up, honest. Some Homicide cops—"

"It *felt* like being stood up. I waited in the newspaper office until a quarter to eight, God knows why. Why didn't you call?"

"They wouldn't let me use the phone." Kling paused. "Besides, I didn't know how I could reach you."

Claire was silent.

"Claire?"

"I'm here," she said wearily.

"Can I see you tomorrow? We'll spend the day together. I'm off tomorrow."

Again there was silence.

"Claire?"

"I heard you."

"Well?"

"Bert, why don't we call it quits, huh? Let's consider what happened tonight an ill omen, and just forget the whole thing, shall we?"

"No," he said.

"Bert—"

"No! I'll pick you up at noon, all right?"

Silence.

"Claire?"

"All right. Yes," she said. "Noon."

"I'll explain then. I . . . I got into a little trouble."

"All right."

"Noon?"

"Yes."

"Claire?"

"Yes?"

"Good night, Claire."

"Good night, Bert."

"I'm sorry I woke you."

"That's all right. I'd just dozed off, anyway."

"Well . . . good night, Claire."

"Good night, Bert."

He wanted to say more, but he heard the click of the receiver being replaced in the cradle. He sighed, left the phone booth, and ordered a steak with mushrooms,

French fried onions, two baked potatoes, a huge salad with Roquefort dressing, and a glass of milk. He finished off the meal with three more glasses of milk and a slab of chocolate cream pie.

On the way out of the restaurant, he bought a candy bar.

Then he went home to sleep.

16

A common and much believed fallacy in popular literature is the one which links romantic waiters with starry-eyed couples who are obviously in love. The waiter hovers over the table, suggesting special dishes ("Per'aps the pheasant under ground glass for ze lady, yas?"), kissing his fingers, or wringing his hands against his chest while his heart bursts with romance.

Bert Kling had been in a good many restaurants in the city, as boy and man, with a good many young ladies ranging from the plain to the beautiful. He had come to the conclusion a long while back that most waiters in most restaurants had nothing more romantic on their minds than an order of scrambled eggs with lox.

He did not for a moment believe that he and Claire looked starry-eyed with love, but they were without doubt a nice-enough-looking couple, and they were in a fashionable restaurant which overlooked the River Harb, high atop one of the city's better-known hotels. And, even discounting the absence of the starry-eyes (which he was fast coming to believe were nothing more than a Jon Whitcomb creation—ah, once a man begins to doubt . . .), he felt that any waiter with more than a stone for a heart should have recognized and aided the fumbling and primitive ritual of two people who were trying to get to know each other.

The day, by any standards, had not been what Kling would have called a rousing success.

He had planned on a picnic in Bethtown, with its attendant ferry ride from Isola across the river. Rain had destroyed that silly notion.

He had drippingly called for Claire at twelve on the dot. The rain had given her a "horrible headache." Would he mind if they stayed indoors for a little while, just until the Empirin took hold?

Kling did not mind.

Claire had put some good records into the record player, and then had lapsed into a heavy silence which he attributed to the throbbing headache. The rain had oozed against the window panes, streaking the city outside. The music had oozed from the record player—Bach's *Brandenburg Concerto No. 5 in D,* Strauss' *Don Quixote,* Franck's *Psyche.*

Kling almost fell asleep.

They left the apartment at two. The rain had let up somewhat, but it had put a knife-edge on the air, and they sloshed along in a sullen, uncommunicative silence, hating the rain with common enmity, but somehow having allowed the rain to build a solid wedge between them. When Kling suggested a movie, Claire accepted the offer eagerly.

The movie was terrible.

The feature was called *Apache Undoing,* or some such damn thing, and it starred hordes of painted Hollywood extras who screeched and whooped down upon a small band of blue-clothed soldiers. The handful of soldiers fought off the wily Apaches until almost the end of the movie. By this time, the hordes flung against the small, tired band must have numbered in the tens of thousands. With five minutes to go in the film, another small handful of soldiers arrived, leaving Kling with the distinct impression that the war would go on for another two hours in a subsequent film to be titled *Son of Apache Undoing.*

The second film on the bill was about a little girl whose mother and father are getting divorced. The little girl goes with them to Reno—Dad conveniently has business there at the same time Mom must establish residence—and through an unvarying progression of mincing postures and bright-eyed, smirking little-girl facial expressions, convinces Mom and Dad to stay together eternally and live in connubial bliss with their mincing, bright-eyed, smirking little smart-assed daughter.

They left the theater bleary-eyed. It was six o'clock.

Kling suggested a drink and dinner. Claire, probably in self-defense, agreed that a drink and dinner would be just dandy along about now.

And so they sat in the restaurant high atop one of the city's better-known hotels, and they looked through the huge windows which faced the river; and across the river there was a sign.

The sign first said: SPRY.

Then it said: SPRY FOR FRYING.

Then it said: SPRY FOR BAKING.

Then it said, again: SPRY.

"What'll you drink?" Kling asked.

"A whisky sour, I think," Claire said.

"No cognac?"

"Later maybe."

The waiter came over to the table. He looked as romantic as Adolf Hitler.

"Something to drink, sir?" he asked.

"A whisky sour, and a Martini."

"Lemon peel, sir?"

"Olive," Kling said.

"Thank you, sir. Would you care to see a menu now?"

"We'll wait until after we've had our drinks, thank you. All right, Claire?"

"Yes, fine," she said.

They sat in silence. Kling looked through the windows.

SPRY FOR FRYING.

"Claire?"

"Yes?"

SPRY FOR BAKING.

"It's been a bust, hasn't it?"

"Please, Bert."

"The rain . . . and that lousy movie. I didn't want it to be this way. I wanted—"

"I knew this would happen, Bert. I tried to tell you, didn't I? Didn't I try to warn you off? Didn't I tell you I was the dullest girl in the world? Why did you insist, Bert? Now you make me feel like a—like a—"

"I don't want you to feel *any* way," he said. "I was only going to suggest that we—we start afresh. From now. Forgetting everything that's—that's happened."

"Oh, what's the use?" Claire said.

The waiter came with their drinks. "Whisky sour for the lady?" he asked.

"Yes."

He put the drinks on the table. Kling lifted the Martini glass.

"To a new beginning," he said.

"If you want to waste a drink," she answered, and she drank.

"About last night—" he started.

"I thought this was to be a new beginning."

"I wanted to explain. I got picked up by two Homicide cops and taken to their lieutenant who warned me to keep away from the Jeannie Paige potato."

"Are you going to?"

"Yes, of course." He paused. "I'm curious, I admit, but . . ."

"I understand."

"Claire," he said evenly, "what the hell is the matter with you?"

"Nothing."

"Where do you go when you retreat?"

"What?"

"Where do you . . . ?"

"I didn't think it showed. I'm sorry."

"It shows," Kling said. "Who was he?"

Claire looked up sharply. "You're a better detective than I realized."

"It doesn't take much detection," he said. There was a sad undertone to his voice now, as if her confirmation of his suspicions had suddenly taken all the fight out of him. "I don't mind your carrying a torch. Lots of girls—"

"It's not that," she interrupted.

"Lots of girls do," he continued. "A guy drops them cold, or else it just peters out the way romances sometimes—"

"It's not that!" she said sharply, and when he looked across the table at her, her eyes filmed with tears.

"Hey, listen, I—"

"Please, Bert, I don't want to—"

"But you said it *was* a guy. You said—"

"All right," she answered. "All right, Bert." She bit down on her lip. "All right, there was a guy. And I was

135

crazy in love with him. I was seventeen—just like Jeannie Paige—and he was nineteen."

Kling waited. Claire lifted her drink and drained the glass. She swallowed hard, and then sighed and Kling watched her, waiting.

"I met him at Club Tempo. We hit it off right away —Do you know how such things happen, Bert? It happened that way with us. We made a lot of plans, big plans. We were young, and we were strong, and we were in love."

"I—I don't understand," he said.

"He was killed in Korea."

Across the river, the sign blared, SPRY FOR FRYING.

The table was very silent. Claire stared at the tablecloth. Kling folded his hands nervously.

"So don't ask me why I go down to the Tempo and make a fool of myself with kids like Hud and Tommy. I'm looking for *him* all over again, Bert, can't you see that? I'm looking for his face, and his youth, and—"

Cruelly, Bert Kling said, "You won't find him."

"I—"

"You won't find him. You're a fool for trying. He's dead and buried. He's—"

"I don't want to listen to you," Claire said. "Take me home, please."

"No," he said. He's dead and buried, and *you're* burying yourself alive, you're making a martyr of yourself, you're wearing a widow's weeds at twenty! What the hell's the matter with you? Don't you know that people die every day? Don't you know?"

"Shut up!" she said.

"Don't you know you're killing yourself? Over a kid's puppy love—over a—"

"Shut up!" she said again, and this time her voice was on the verge of hysteria, and some of the diners around them turned at her outburst.

"Okay!" Kling said tightly. "Okay, bury yourself! Bury your beauty, and try to hide your sparkle! Wear black every day of the week for all I give a damn! But I think you're a phony! I think you're a fourteen-carat phony!" He paused, and then said angrily, "Let's get the hell out of this goldfish bowl!"

He started to rise, signaling for the waiter at the same time. Claire sat motionless opposite him. And then, quite suddenly, she began to cry. The tears started slowly at first, forcing their way past clenched eyelids, trickling silently down her cheeks. And then her shoulders began to heave, and she sat as still as a stone, her hands clasped in her lap, her shoulders heaving, sobbing silently while the tears coursed down her face. He had never seen such honest misery before. He turned his face away. He did not want to watch her.

"You are ready to order, sir?" the waiter asked, sidling up to the table.

"Two more of the same," Bert said. The waiter started off, and he caught at his arm. "No. Change the whisky sour to a double shot of Canadian Club."

"Yes, sir," the waiter said, padding off.

"I don't want another drink," Claire muttered.

"You'll have one."

"I don't want one." She erupted into tears again, and this time Kling watched her. She sobbed steadily for several moments, and then the tears stopped as suddenly as they had begun, leaving her face looking as clean as a city street does after a sudden summer storm.

"I'm sorry," she said.

"Don't be."

"I should have cried a long time ago."

"Yes."

The waiter brought the drinks. Kling lifted his glass. "To a new beginning," he said.

Claire studied him. It took her a long while to reach for the double hooker before her. Finally, her hand closed around the glass. She lifted it and touched the rim of Kling's glass. "To a new beginning," she said. She threw off the shot quickly.

"That's strong," she said.

"It'll do you good."

"Yes. I'm sorry, Bert. I shouldn't have burdened you with my troubles."

"Offhand, can you think of anyone who'd accept them so readily?"

"No," she said immediately. She smiled tiredly.

"That's better."

She looked across at him as if she were seeing him for

the first time. The tears had put a sparkle into her eyes. "It—it may take time, Bert," she said. Her voice came from a long way off.

"I've got all the time in the world," he said. And then, almost afraid she would laugh at him, he added, "All I've been doing is killing time, Claire, waiting for you to come along."

She seemed ready to cry again. He reached across the table and covered her hand with his.

"You . . . you're very good, Bert," she said, her voice growing thin, the way a voice does before it collapses into tears. "You're good, and kind, and gentle, and you're quite beautiful, do you know that? I . . . I think you're very beautiful."

"You should see me when my hair is combed," he said, smiling, squeezing her hand.

"I'm not joking," she said. "You always think I'm joking, and you really shouldn't because I'm—I'm a serious girl."

"I know."

"So—"

He shifted his position abruptly, grimacing.

"Is something wrong?" she asked, suddenly concerned.

"No. This goddamn pistol." He shifted again.

"Pistol?"

"Yes. In my back pocket. We have to carry them, you know. Even off duty."

"Not really? A gun? You have a gun in your pocket?"

"Sure."

She leaned closer to him. Her eyes were clear now, as if they had never known tears or sadness. They sparkled with interest. "May I see it?"

"Sure." He reached down, unbuttoned his jacket, and then pulled the gun with its leather holster from his hip pocket. He put it on the table. "Don't touch it, or it'll go off in your face."

"It looks menacing."

"It *is* menacing. I'm the deadest shot in the 87th Precinct."

"Are you really?"

" 'Kling the King,' they call me."

She laughed suddenly.

138

"I can shoot any damn elephant in the world at a distance of three feet," Kling expanded. Her laugh grew. He watched her laughing. She seemed unaware of the transformation.

"Do you know what I feel like doing?" he said.

"What?"

"I feel like taking this gun and shooting out that goddamn Spry sign across the river."

"Bert," she said, "Bert," and she put her other hand over his, so that three hands formed a pyramid on the table. Her face grew very serious. "Thank you, Bert. Thank you so very, very much."

He didn't know what to say. He felt embarrassed and stupid and happy and very big. He felt about eighty feet tall.

"What—what are you doing tomorrow?" he asked.

"Nothing. What are you doing tomorrow?"

"I'm calling Molly Bell to explain why I can't snoop around any more. And then I'm stopping by at your place, and we're going on a picnic. *If* the sun is shining."

"The sun'll be shining, Bert."

"I know it will," he said.

She leaned forward suddenly and kissed him, a quick, sudden kiss that fleetingly touched his mouth and then was gone. She sat back again, seeming very unsure of herself, seeming like a frightened little girl at her first party. "You—you must be patient," she said.

"I will," he promised.

The waiter suddenly appeared. The waiter was smiling. He coughed discreetly. Kling watched him in amazement.

"I thought," the waiter said gently, "perhaps a little candlelight at the table, sir? The lady will look even more lovely by candlelight."

"The lady looks lovely just as she is," Kling said.

The waiter seemed disappointed. "But . . ."

"But the candlelight, certainly," Kling said. "By all means, the candlelight."

The waiter beamed. "Ah, yes, sir. Yes, sir. And then we will order, yes? I have some suggestions, sir, whenever you're ready." He paused, his smile lighting his face. "It's a beautiful night, sir, isn't it?"

"It's a wonderful night," Claire answered.

17

Sometimes, they crack open like litchi nuts.

You struggle with something that seems to be a Brazil nut, poking at the diamond-hard exterior, yearning to get at the meat—and suddenly it's a litchi nut with a fragile, paper-thin skin, and it bursts open under the slightest pressure of your fingers.

It happened that way with Willis and Havilland.

The Three Aces that Sunday afternoon, September 24, had barely begun picking up business after its late opening. There were a few drinkers at the bar, but the tables were empty, and both the snookers table and the bowling pinball machine were empty of players. The bar was a run-down joint with three playing cards painted on the mirror: the ace of clubs, the ace of hearts, and the ace of spades. The fourth ace was nowhere visible. Judging from the looks of the bartender, it was probably up his sleeve, together with a fifth ace.

Willis and Havilland took stools at the end of the bar. The bartender lingered with the drinkers at the opposite end of the bar for a few minutes, then slouchingly pulled himself away from the conversation, walked to Willis and Havilland, and said, "Yep?"

Havilland threw the match folder onto the bar. "This yours?"

The bartender studied it at great length. The identical three aces on the mirror fronted the match folder. The name Three Aces was plastered on the cardboard in red letters a half inch high. The bartender nonetheless took his time.

At last, he said, "Yep."

"How long have you been stocking them?" Willis asked.

"Why?"

"We're police officers," Havilland said wearily. He reached into his pocket for his shield.

"Save it," the bartender said. "I can smell law at sixty paces."

"Is that how you got your nose broken?" Havilland asked, clenching his fists on the bar top.

The bartender touched his nose. "I used to box," he said. "What's with the matches?"

"How long have you stocked them?"

"About three months. It was a big bargain. There's this kid in the neighborhood, sells Christmas cards and like that. Came around saying the matches would give the joint a little class. So I tumbled. Ordered a coupla gross." The bartender shrugged. "Didn't do no harm, as I can see. What's the beef?"

"No beef," Willis said. "Routine check."

"On what? Matchbooks?"

"Yeah," Havilland said. "On matchbooks. Do you sell cigarettes?"

"Only in the machine." The bartender indicated the vending apparatus in the corner near the door.

"You stock these matches in the machine?"

"No. We keep 'em on the bar in a small box. Anybody runs out of matches, he comes up and grabs himself a book. Why? What's so important with the matches?"

"We'll ask the questions," Havilland said.

"I'm only trying to help, officer," the bartender said. His voice conveyed the distinct impression that he would have liked nothing better than to punch Havilland in the mouth.

"Then anyone who drinks here can walk up to the bar and help himself to the matches, that right?" Willis asked.

"Yep," the bartender said. "Makes it homey, don't you think?"

"Mister," Havilland said evenly, "you better wipe that wise-guy smirk off your voice, or something's gonna make *you* homely."

"Cops have always scared me," the bartender said dryly, "ever since I was a wee babe."

"If you're looking for a fight, pal," Havilland said, "you picked the right cop."

"I'm lookin' to mind my own business," the bartender said.

"I'd hate like hell to have a judge decide on whose

word to take in a 'resisting an officer' case." Havilland persisted.

"I ain't fighting, and I ain't resisting nothing," the bartender replied. "So cool off. You want a beer?"

"I'll have a Scotch," Havilland said.

"That figures," the bartender drawled. "How about you?" he asked Willis.

"Nothing," Willis said.

"Come on," the bartender egged. It's just like grabbing an apple from the pushcart."

"When you're ready for that fight," Willis said, "you've got two of us now."

"Whenever I fought, I got paid for it," the bartender said. "I don't believe in exhibition bouts."

"Especially when you know your ass'll be spread over six counties," Havilland said.

"Sure," the bartender said. He poured a hooker of Scotch and then slid the glass to Havilland.

"You know most of your customers?" Willis asked.

"The steadies, sure."

The door opened, and a woman in a faded green sweater walked into the bar, looked around, and then sat at a table near the door. The bartender glanced at her.

"She's a lush," he said. "She'll sit there until somebody offers to buy her a drink. I'd kick her out, but I feel Christian on Sunday."

"It shows all over you," Havilland said.

"What is it you guys want, anyway?" the bartender asked. "The fight? Is that what this is all about?"

"What fight?" Willis asked.

"We had a rhubarb here week or so ago. Listen, don't snow me. What have you got up your sleeve? Disorderly conduct? You figure on yanking my license?"

"You're doing all the talking so far," Willis said.

The bartender sighed wearily. "All right, what'll it cost?"

"Oh, this man lives dangerously," Havilland said. "Are you attempting to bribe us, you son of a btich?"

"I was talking about the price of the new Lincoln Continental," the bartender said. "I asked what it'll cost." He paused. "A hundred, two hundred? How much?"

"Do I look like a two-hundred-dollar cop?" Havilland asked.

"I'm a two-hundred-dollar bartender," the bartender said. "That's the limit. The goddamn fight was over in about two seconds flat."

"What kind of a fight?" Willis asked.

"You mean you don't know?"

"Put your money back in your sock," Willis said. "This isn't a shakedown. Tell us about the fight."

The bartender seemed relieved. "You sure you don't want a drink, Officer?" he asked.

"The fight," Willis said.

"It was nothing," the bartender said. Couple of guys got hot-headed, and wham! One took a swing at the other, the other swung back, and I came over and busted it up. That's all."

"Who swung at who?" Willis asked.

"These two characters. What the hell's the name of the little guy? I don't remember. The bigger guy is called Jack. He comes in here a lot."

"Jack, huh?"

"Yeah. Nice guy, except he's a little weird. So him and this little guy were watching the rassling on TV, and I guess Jack said something the little guy didn't like—about one of the rasslers, you know? So the little guy hauls off and pops Jack. So Jack takes a swing at the little guy, and that's when I came over. Big fight, huh?"

"And you broke it up?"

"Sure. I tell you, the funny thing about this whole business was that the little guy come out of it better than Jack." The bartender chuckled. "He really gave him a shot, I swear. You wouldn't think a little guy could pack such a wallop."

"I'll bet Jack was surprised," Willis said, losing interest.

"Surprised? I'll say he was. Especially when he took a gander in the mirror. That little son of a bitch gave him a shiner like I never saw in my life."

"Too bad for Jack," Willis said. "About your other customers. Have you ever heard any of them talking about—"

"Boy, that shiner was a beaut! Hell, Jack had to wear sunglasses for about a week afterward."

The lush sitting at the table near the door coughed. Willis kept staring at the bartender.

"What did you say?" he asked.

"Jack," the bartender said. "Had to wear these sunglasses. To hide the shiner, you know. It was a beautiful shiner, I mean it. Like a rainbow."

"This Jack," Willis said. He could feel the tenseness of Havilland alongside him. "Does he smoke?"

"Jack? Yeah, sure. He smokes."

"What brand?"

"Brand? Jesus, you must think I'm a—Wait a minute, the red package, what's the red package?"

"Pall Mall?"

"Yep. That's his brand."

"You're sure?"

"I think so. Listen, I didn't go around taking a picture of what he smokes. I think it's Pall Mall. Why?"

"You're sure his name is Jack?" Havilland asked. It isn't something else?"

"Jack," the bartender said, nodding.

"Think. Are you sure his name is Jack?"

"I'm positive. Listen, don't I know him? For God's sake, he's been coming in here for years. Don't you think I know Jack Clifford?"

Jack Clifford came into the Three Aces at three-fifteen that afternoon. The woman in the green sweater still sat at the table near the door. The bartender nodded when he entered, and Willis and Havilland moved off their stools quickly and intercepted him as he walked toward the bar.

"Jack Clifford?" Willis asked.

"Yeah?"

"Police officers," Havilland said. You're coming with us."

"Hey, what for?" Clifford said. He pulled his arm away from Havilland.

"Assault and suspicion of murder," Willis snapped. He was running his hands over Clifford's body, frisking him quickly and efficiently.

"He's clea—" he started, and Clifford broke for the door.

"Get him!" Willis shouted. Havilland was reaching

144

for his gun. Clifford didn't look back. He kept his eyes glued to the entrance doorway, and he ran like a bat out of hell, and then he fell flat on his face.

He looked up from the floor instantly, startled. The lush still sat at the table, one leg spread out in front of her. Clifford looked at the leg which had tripped him, looked at it as if he wanted to cut it off at the hipbone. He was scrambling to his feet when Havilland reached him. He kicked out at Havilland, but Havilland was a cop with big hands, and Havilland enjoyed using those hands. He scooped Clifford off the floor and rammed his first into Clifford's face. Clifford staggered back against the door, and then collapsed on the floor. He sat there shaking his head while Havilland put the cuffs on him.

"Did you enjoy your trip?" Havilland asked pleasantly.

"Go to hell," Clifford said. "If it wasn't for that old drunken bag you'd never have got me."

"Ah, but we did." Havilland said. "Get up!"

Clifford got to his feet. Willis came over and took his arm. He turned to the bartender. "Thanks," he said.

Together, the three men started out of the bar. Havilland stopped just inside the doorway, at the table with the lush. The woman raised her head and studied him with alcohol-soaked eyes.

Havilland smiled, bowed, and swept one gorilla-like arm across his waist.

"Havilland thanks you, madam," he said.

He admitted he had committed a total of thirty-four muggings in the past year. Fourteen of his victims had complained to the police. His last victim had turned out to be, of all goddamn things, a policewoman.

He denied flatly that he had assaulted and murdered Jeannie Paige.

They booked, mugged, and printed him—and then they sat with him in the Interrogation Room at the 87th and tried to break down his story. There were four cops in the room with him. Willis, Havilland, Meyer, and Lieutenant Byrnes. Were it not for the presence of the lieutenant, Havilland would have been practicing his favorite indoor sport. At it was, his barrage was confined to words alone.

"We're talking about the night of September fourteenth. That was a Thursday night. Now think about it a little, Clifford," Meyer said.

"I'm thinking. I got an alibi a mile long for that night."

"What were you doing?" Willis asked.

"I was sitting up with a sick friend."

"Don't get smart!" Byrnes said.

"I swear to God, it's the truth. Listen, you got me on eight thousand counts of assault. Why're you trying to stick me with a murder rap?"

"Shut your goddamn mouth and answer the questions," Havilland said, contradicting himself.

"I am answering the questions. I was with a sick friend. The guy had ptomaine poisoning or something. I was with him all night."

"What night was this?"

"September fourteenth," Clifford said.

"How come you remember the date?"

"I was supposed to go bowling."

"With whom?"

"This friend of mine."

"Which friend?"

"What's your friend's name?"

"Where were you going bowling?"

"His name is Davey," Clifford said.

"Davey what?"

"Davey Crockett, Clifford? Come on, Clifford."

"Davey Lowenstein. He's a Jew. You gonna hang me for that?"

"Where does he live?"

"Base Avenue.

"Where on Base?"

"Near Seventh."

"What's his name?"

"Davey Lowenstein. I told you already."

"Where were you going bowling?"

"The Cozy Alleys."

"Downtown?"

"Yes."

"Where downtown?"

"Jesus, you're mixing me up."

"What'd your friend eat?"

"Did he have a doctor?"

"Where'd you say he lived?"

"Who says he had ptomaine poisoning?"

"He lives on Base, I told you. Base and Seventh."

"Check that, Meyer," Lieutenant Byrnes said. Meyer quickly left the room.

"Did he have a doctor?"

"No."

"Then how do you know it was ptomaine?"

"He said it felt like ptomaine."

"How long were you with him?"

"I went by for him at eight. That was when I was supposed to pick him up. The alley we were going to is on Division."

"He was sick in bed?"

"Yeah."

"Who answered the door?"

"He did."

"I thought he was sick in bed."

"He was. He got out of bed to answer the door."

"What time was this?"

"Eight."

"You said eight-thirty."

"No, it was eight. Eight, I said."

"What happened?"

"He said he was sick, said he had ptomaine, said he couldn't go with me. To the bowling alley, I mean."

"Then what?"

"He told me to go without him."

"Did you?"

"No, I stayed with him all night."

"Until when?"

"Until the next morning. All night, I stayed with him."

"Until what time?"

"All night."

"WHAT TIME?"

"About nine in the morning. We had eggs together."

"What happened to his ptomaine?"

"He was all right in the morning."

"Did he sleep?"

"What?"

"Did he sleep at all that night?"

"No."

147

"What'd you do?"

"We played checkers."

"Who?"

"Me and Davey."

"What time did you stop playing checkers?"

"About four in the morning."

"Did he go to sleep then?"

"No."

"What did he do?"

"We began telling jokes. I was trying to take his mind off his stomach."

"You told jokes until nine the next morning?"

"No, until eight. We started breakfast at eight."

"What'd you eat?"

"Eggs."

"What bowling alley did you say that was?"

"The Cozy—"

"Where's it located?"

"On Division."

"What time did you get to Davey's house?"

"Eight o'clock."

"Why'd you kill Jeannie Paige?"

"I didn't. Jesus, the newspapers are killing *me!* I didn't go anywhere near the Hamilton Bridge."

"You mean that night?"

"That night, any night. I don't even know that cliff they wrote about. I thought cliffs were out west."

"Which cliff?"

"Where the girl was found."

"Which girl?"

"Jeannie Paige."

"Did she scream? Is that why you killed her?"

"She didn't scream."

"What did she do?"

"She didn't do nothing! I wasn't there! How do I know what she did?"

"But you beat up your other victims, didn't you?"

"Yes. You got me on that, okay."

"You son of a bitch, we've got a thumbprint on the sunglasses you dropped. We'll get you on that, so why don't you tell us about it?"

"There's nothing to tell. My friend was sick. I don't

148

know Jeannie Paige. I don't know that cliff. Lock me up. Try me on assault. I didn't kill that girl!"

"Who did?"

"I don't know."

"You did!"

"No."

"Why'd you kill her?"

"I didn't kill her!"

The door opened. Meyer Meyer came into the room. "I called this Lowenstein character," he said.

"Yeah?"

"The story is true. Clifford was with him all that night."

When the comparison tests were made with Clifford's thumbprints and the single print found on the sunglasses, there was no longer any doubt. The prints did not match.

Whatever else Jack Clifford had done, he had not murdered Jeannie Paige.

18

There was only Molly Bell to call.

Once he'd done that, he could leave the Jeannie Paige thing with a clear conscience. He had tried, he had honestly tried. And his efforts had led him into the jealously guarded realm of Homicide North, where he'd damn near wound up minus a shield and a uniform.

So now he would call her, and he would explain how useless he was, and he would apologize, and that would be the end of it.

Sitting in an armchair in his furnished room, Kling pulled the telephone toward him. He reached into his back pocket for his wallet, opened it, and then began leafing through the cards and scraps of paper, looking for the address and telephone number Bell had given him so long ago. He spread the cards on the end table. Christ, the collection of junk a man can. . . .

He looked at the date on a raffle ticket. The drawing had been held three months ago. There was a girl's name and telephone number on a match folder. He didn't remember the girl at all. There was an entrance card to a discount house. There was the white card Claire had given him to explain Jeannie's childish handwriting. He put the card on the table so that the reverse side showed, the side reading "Club Tempo, 1812 Klausner Street."

And then he found the scrap of paper Peter Bell had handed to him, and he put that face up on the table alongside the other cards, and he reached for the phone receiver, studying the number at the same time.

And suddenly he remembered what he'd seen in the street at the first subway stop. He dropped the receiver.

He put all the cards and scraps of paper back into his wallet.

Then he put on his coat.

He was waiting for a murderer.

He had taken a train uptown, and he had got off at the first stop he'd visited earlier that week, and he was in the street now, standing alongside a Police Department sign, and waiting for a murderer, the murderer of Jeannie Paige.

The night had turned cold, and there weren't many people in the street. The men's clothing store was closed, and the Chinese restaurant belched steam into the air from a vent on the side of the building. A few people straggled into the movie house.

He waited, and when the car pulled up, he put one hand on the police sign alongside him and waited for the door to open.

The man came out of the car and started walking toward the curb. He was not a bad-looking man. He had even white teeth and an enviable cleft in his chin. He was tall and muscularly built. There was only one bad feature on his face.

"Hello," Kling said.

The man looked up, startled. His eyes fled to Kling's face and then to the sign alongside Kling.

The sign read:

150

Peter Bell said, "Bert? Is that you, Bert?"

Kling stepped into the light. "It's me, Peter," he said.

Bell looked confused. "Hi," he said. "What—what brings you down here?"

"You, Peter."

"Well, good. Always glad to have a friend—" He stopped. "Listen, you want a cup of coffee or something? Take the chill off?"

"No, Peter," Kling said.

"Well . . . uh . . . what is it?"

"I'm taking you with me, Peter. Up to the house."

"The house? You mean the precinct?" Bell's brows swooped down. "What for? What's the matter with you, Bert?"

"For the murder of your sister-in-law, Jeannie Paige," Kling said.

Bell stared at Kling and then smiled tremulously. "You're kidding."

"I'm not kidding, Peter."

"Well, you . . . you must be kidding! I never heard such a stupid—"

"You're a son of a bitch!" Kling said vehemently. "I ought to beat you black and blue and then—"

"Listen, hold it. Just hold—"

"Hold, crap!" Kling shouted. "You egotistical son of a bitch, did you think I was an absolute moron? Is that why you picked me to begin with? A rookie cop? A cop who wouldn't know his ass from his elbow? Is that why you picked me to placate Molly? Bring a cop around, show the little woman you're trying, and that would make everything all right, wouldn't it? What was it you said, Peter? *That way, Molly'll be happy. If I bring a cop around, she'll be happy.* Isn't that what you said, you bastard?"

"Yes, but—"

"You read six newspapers a day! You stumbled on the item about your old pal Bert Kling being discharged from the hospital and resting up, so you figured he was the perfect chump. Bring him around, get Molly off your neck, and then you'd be free to—"

"Listen, Bert, you've got this all wrong. You're—"

"I've got it all right, Peter! My coming around would have been the end of it, but something else came up, didn't it? Jeannie told you she was pregnant. Jeannie told you she was carrying your child!"

"No, listen—"

"Don't 'No' me, Peter! Isn't that what happened? She said she had an appointment the night I talked to her. Was the appointment with you? Did she drop her bombshell then? Did she tell you and then give you time to mull it over for the next day, give you time to work out the way you were going to kill her?"

Bell was silent for a long time. Then he said, "I didn't see her that Wednesday night. Her appointment wasn't with me."

"Who then?"

"A doctor." Bell swallowed. "I saw her on Thursday. She met me here, at the the hack stand, the way she always did. Bert, this isn't what you think, believe me. I loved her, I loved her."

"I'll just bet you did! I'll bet you adored her, Peter, I'll bet you—"

"Why does marriage go stale?" Bell said plaintively. "Why does it have to go stale, Bert? Why couldn't Molly have stayed the way she was? Young and fresh and pretty . . . like—"

"Like Jeannie? *She looks just the way Molly looked when she was that age.*' That's what you told me, Peter. Remember?"

"Yes! She was Molly all over again, and I watched her growing up, and I—I fell in love with her. Is that so hard to understand? Is it so goddamn difficult to understand that a man could fall in love?"

"That's not the hard part, Peter."

"What then? What? What can you—"

"You don't kill somebody you love," Kling said.

"She was hysterical!" Bell said. "I met her here, and we drove, and she told me the doctor had said she was pregnant. She said she was going to tell Molly all about it! How could I let her do that?"

"So you killed her."

"I—we parked on the River Highway. She walked ahead of me, to the top of the cliff. I—I had a monkey wrench with me. I—I carry one in the cab, in case of burglaries, in case of—"

"Peter, you didn't have to . . ."

Bell wasn't listening to Kling. Bell was reliving the night of September 14. "I . . . I hit her twice. She fell backwards, rolling, rolling. Then the bushes stopped her, and she lay there like a broken doll. I . . . I went back to the cab. I was ready to drive away when I remembered the newspaper stories about Clifford the mugger. I . . . I carried a cheap pair of sunglasses in the glove compartment. I . . . I took them out and broke one lens in the cab, so that it would look like the glasses were broken in a struggle and then fell over the side of the cliff. I went back up the cliff again, and she still lay there, broken and bleeding, and I threw the glasses down, and then I rode off, and I left her there."

"Was it you who sicked Homicide North on me, Peter?"

"Yes." Bell's voice was very low. "I—I didn't know how much you knew. I couldn't take any chances."

"No." Kling paused. "You took a chance the first night you met me, Peter."

"What?"

"You wrote your address and phone number for me. And the handwriting is the same as the writing on a card Jeannie took to Club Tempo."

"I knew the club from when I was a kid," Bell said. "I figured—as a blind, a cover-up—to throw Molly off if she got wise. Bert, I—" He stopped. "You can't prove anything with that handwriting. So what if I—?"

"We've got all the proof we need, Peter."

"You haven't got a damn—"

"We've got your thumbprint on the sunglasses."

Bell was silent again. And then, as if the words were torn bleeding and raw from him, he shouted, "I loved her!"

"And she loved you, and the poor damn kid had to keep her first love hidden like a thief. And like a thief, Peter, you stole her life. What I said still goes. You're a son of a bitch."

"Bert, look, she's dead now. What difference does it make? Can't we—?"

"No."

"Bert, how can I tell this to Molly? Do you know what this'll do to her? Bert, how can I tell her? Bert, give me a break, please. How can I tell her?"

Bert Kling looked at Bell quite coldly. "You made your bed," he said at last. "Come on."

19

On Monday morning, September 25, Steve Carella burst into the Squad Room, raring to go.

"Where the hell is everybody?" he shouted. "Where's my welcoming committee?"

"Well, well," Havilland said, "look who's back."

"The hero returning from the Trojan war," Meyer cracked.

"How was it, boy?" Temple asked.

"Wonderful," Carella said. "Jesus, it's wonderful in the Poconos this time of year."

"It's wonderful *any*where," Meyer said. "Haven't you heard?"

"You're a bunch of lewd bastards," Carella said. "I knew it all along, but this confirms it."

"You're one of us," Meyer said. "We are your brothers."

"Brother!" Carella said. "So what've you been doing for the past month? Sitting on your duffs and collecting salaries?"

"Oh," Meyer said, "few things been going on."

"Tell him about the cats," Temple prompted.

"What cats?" Carella said.

"I'll tell you later," Meyer said patiently.

"We had a homicide," Havilland said.

"Yeah?"

"Yeah," Temple said. "We also got a new Detective 3rd/Grade."

"Yeah?" Carella said. "A transfer?"

"Nope. A promotion. Up from the ranks."

"Who?"

"Bert Kling. You know him?"

"Sure I do. Good for Bert. What'd he do? Rescue the commissioner's wife?"

"Oh, nothing much," Meyer said. "Just sat on his duff and collected his salary."

"So how's married life?" Havilland asked.

"Wonderful."

"These cats George was talking about," Meyer said.

"Yeah?"

"One hell of a thing, believe me. One of the roughest cases the 33rd has ever had."

"No kidding?" Carella said. He walked over to Havilland's desk and helped himself to the coffee container there. The room seemed very warm and very friendly, and he suddenly did not regret being back on the job.

"Damnedest thing," Meyer said patiently. "They had this guy, you see, who was going around kidnapping cats."

Carella sipped at his coffee. The sunlight streamed through the meshed windows. Outside, the city was coming to life.

Another workday was beginning.

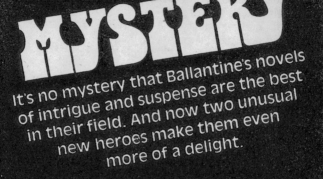

Praise for *The Templar Legacy*

"Steve Berry is on a roll. . . . His most readable book yet. Berry is one of those authors who can blend history and adventure and satisfy both audiences, and he does so with precision in his latest story."
—*Newton Citizen*

"[An] extraordinary work . . . sure to pique the interest of readers who favor suspense, ancient rites, clandestine societies, and lost treasures."
—*The Oklahoman*

"Berry's latest is simultaneously a history lesson and a spellbinding mystery. Danger is ever-present, and the twists culminate in a breathtaking finale."
—*Romantic Times*

"Fascinating and impossible to put down."
—*Record-Courier*

"Berry provides *Da Vinci Code*–type suspense about a fascinating ancient order."
—*OK Magazine*

Once again, Berry takes an unsolved historical mystery . . . and whips it into an action-packed thriller. This is the first of three books to feature Cotton Malone, and I don't plan to miss a single one."
—*Kingston Observer*

Also by Steve Berry

The Amber Room
The Romanov Prophecy
The Third Secret
The Alexandria Link